I AM BAYBIE

*I Am Baybie: Based on the True Story of the Reverend Baybie Hoover
and Her Friend and Deaconess of Music Virginia Brown*
Copyright © 2013 Bill Schubart

Published in April 2013 by Magic Hill Press LLC, 144 Magic Hill Road,
Hinesburg, VT 05461
ISBN: 978-0-9834852-9-2
Library of Congress: 2012924085

Book Design: Alex Ching
Photography: Ann Meuer

Bibliography:
The Lamoille Stories (ISBN 978-1-935052-10-4) White River Press - 2008
Fat People (ISBN 978-0-615-39751-1) Magic Hill Press LLC - 2010
Panhead (ISBN 978-0-9834852-6-1) Magic Hill Press LLC - 2012

Publisher's Cataloging-in-Publication
(Provided by Quality Books, Inc.)
    Schubart, Bill, 1945-
        I am Baybie / Bill Schubart.
        p. cm.
        Includes index.
        ISBN 978-0-9834852-9-2
        1. Hoover, Baybie--Fiction. 2. Brown, Virginia
        (Accordionist)--Fiction. 3. Gospel singers--United
        States--Fiction. 4. Street musicians--United States--
        Fiction. 5. Blind women--United States--Fiction.
        6. Ex-foster children--United States--Fiction. I. Title.

PS3619.C467I26 2013   813'.6
                QBI13-600002

This book is a work of fiction based on the author's acquaintance with the Reverend Baybie Hoover and Virginia Brown, and on a brief field recording by Dr. John Diamond for album liner notes and transcriptions thereof by Priscilla Herdman. The conceit of using "reels" instead of chapters is a fictional device and does not correlate to any actual recordings. The narrative is further informed by a documentary film entitled "A Lady Named Baybie" made by Martha Sandlin in 1980. A recording of their music, Philo 1019, was made in 1976 and is now owned by the Concord Music Group.

Photo Credits: *Cover* Reverend Baybie Hoover in her apartment; *Back cover left to right* Reverend Baybie Hoover, A listener adds to Baybie's tin cup, and Virginia Brown by Ann Meuer. *Back cover bottom* by Peter Miller

For further images and to listen to songs visit IamBaybie.com

I AM BAYBIE

Based on the true story of the
Reverend Baybie Hoover
and her friend and Deaconess
of Music Virginia Brown

A Novel by
Bill Schubart

ACKNOWLEDGMENTS

My gratitude to Hope Mathiessen for her invaluable editorial help. Thanks as well to critical reader, Jericho Parms, who provided invaluable suggestions to shape the manuscript. Ruth Sylvester's deep knowledge of dialect and colloquial speech made her copy-editing invaluable. Aesthetic blessings on Alex Ching who made the book beautiful, using the extraordinary photographs of my black-sheep cousin Ann Meuer, a descendant and acolyte of my great uncle Alfred Stieglitz. Thanks to my wife Kate, a formidable editor, critic, and writer, and my daughter Anna, my most receptive critical reader. Thanks also to Gilbert and Michael Perlman, sage advisors in this time of great change in the publishing industry. Special thanks to Priscilla Herdman and Dr. John Diamond for bringing Baybie and Virginia to my consciousness and to the National Endowment for the Arts for supporting the production of a record of their music, Philo 1019 in 1976.

TABLE OF CONTENTS

My name is Bill. I am a distraction from the story you are about to read. As I get older and watch acquaintances shuffle off to Florida to live among their own and die where it is warm, their names leach slowly from memory and I am left with what matters ... story and the recollection of faces. I see Baybie's rough-hewn but ebullient face and Virginia's pinched smile today as clearly as if we were together in the studio thirty-five years ago.

I am a bit player in Baybie's story ... an extra. I came to know her through another of the extraordinary female singers who recorded for our small folk label, Philo Records: Priscilla Herdman*. She and her friend, Dr. John Diamond**, both shared our interest in folklore and roots music. They made a field recording that piqued my curiosity, so with their help I sought out and met Baybie and Virginia as they sang together on the sidewalk in front of Bloomingdale's on bustling Lexington Avenue in New York City. I, too, was captivated by their unique harmonies and the rarity and depth of their repertoire.

In 1976, Philo recorded an album of Baybie and Virginia (Philo 1019) and several of us became immersed in the narrative of their extraordinarily courageous lives.

Priscilla and John's cassette transcriptions, additional studio tapes of discussions and my recollections of subsequent personal conversations form the basis of this story. I took considerable license in the writing of this first-person narrative. Some of Baybie's own language is verbatim, drawn from Priscilla's transcriptions that appear as liner notes in the album. Though a voluble and forthright woman, Virginia spoke only brief on tape. Little is known about her other than what we hear from Baybie.

I extrapolated additional events from personal conversations with both women. A beautiful documentary film entitled "A Lady Named Baybie" made by Martha Sandlin in 1980, further informs the narrative. The photo-graphs in this book and in the album were a gift from my photographer-cousin, Ann Meuer, who also photographed Eleanor Roosevelt, Louis Armstrong, Martha Graham, and countless anonymous civil rights activists working in Selma, Alabama, in the sixties.

This must, however, be understood as a work of fiction derived from the sparse record of the lives of the Reverend Baybie Hoover and her Deaconess of Music and dear friend, Virginia Brown.

Those of us who knew them have never lost our affection and profound respect for their talent, courage, and joie de vivre in the face of adversity. The echo of their singing endures today.

Bill Schubart, April 2013

I am Baybie. I'm a working woman. I live in a room on West 46th. The agency calls it an SRO. That means "single room occupancy," but I call it my apartment. It's in the Markwell Hotel.

My grandmother used to call me "Baby," and of course she was the only one that ever cared for me when I was a child. I lost her when I was seven and I always liked the name Baby and I just thought, "I didn't have anyone to care for me." I just thought, you know, well maybe people won't be... I mean, I know that people don't mean that they care for me when they say Baby... it just sounds so nice.

What really started it, Virginia and I went to Stouffer's and lots of times Ginger called me Baby, you know, 'cause we'd been close like sisters. It was kind of just a pet name. She'd say, "Baby," so one of the hostesses at Stouffer's said, "So, Baby, would you like some water?" She didn't know my name. And I just thought, "Well, hey, that sounds great; I think I'll just insist that everybody call me Baby."

So, once, Ginger and I spent a night at the Lighthouse and I was spelling it B-a-b-y, just plain "Baby." And the woman said that looked so undignified; you know you're not a baby. I said. "No, I'm not a baby; I'm a lady named Baby." And they said no, your name isn't Baby; it's "Nadine" and "Nadine" is a pretty name. And so the woman interviewing us looked up the name Nadine and she said Nadine means "hope" in Russian. It's a derived from a Russian name, and she said it means "hope," and I says, "Yeah, and that's wonderful," but I says, 'I'm getting tired of just hopin' all the time." I said, "I'm makin' a new start and my name's now Baybie," and I spelled it different like it would be mine.

I work every day for eight hours, six in winter. Virginia Brown, I call her Ginger, is my Deaconess of Music. She sings harmony with me and plays the accordion. She lives downtown. I don't know where exactly. We work for a living. We start every morning when Bloomingdale's opens at 9:00 A.M. and sing until five or sometimes six if our pay is good. In the winter, we quit at dusk, which sometimes is as early as four.

It's harder in winter. Lewis, the doorman at Bloomingdale's is a nice man and lets us take a warming break in the entryway in winter if it's really cold. Negro men used to scare me, but not anymore. I know by their voices if they are Negroes. In Lewis' case, I could tell that he was a good-hearted man with a deep rumbling laughter in his voice. I wish I could see his eyes. People tell me you can tell someone's intentions for you in their eyes, but I hear it in their voice. Once, he gave me some warm coffee from his thermos. He doesn't put sugar in his coffee though and it was bitter, but I thanked him just the same.

Sometimes, if it's really hot in summer, Lewis invites us in to cool off. The air conditioning works even in the foyer between the entry doors. That cool air sure enough feels good when it's hot outside. All Lewis seems to care about is that we don't trouble the customers while we're working.

Lewis likes our music, but says he's not familiar with most of the songs. Negroes come from a different church tradition than Virginia and me. He's a nice man though and always treats us well.

We've been singing outside of Bloomingdale's for twelve years now. When we first started singing here, the security manager tried to chase us off. I showed him how we were on the public sidewalk and never interfered with his boss's customers but he kept shooing us away. Officer Clemens, who walks the beat on Lex. and Third and who we got to know later on, stood up for us, though. He warned us to stay far away from the doors. Later, he told me with a smile in his voice that we had won and even later, Lewis told me that we were a "fixture." I'm not sure I ever knew what he meant, but we've been working here now for twelve years just like all those pretty girls who work inside and we've never had a complaint since. Those that don't like our music just "walk on by" as the radio song goes.

Oh, I sometimes wonder what it looks like inside. I can smell the perfume smells that come out the doors when they open. Lewis jokes that the girls inside sell perfumes and makeup to rich ladies are all too thin for his taste. He says, "I like a little meat on my bone, like you girls have," and then he laughs and laughs in his deep baritone voice. He says the skinny girls help the rich women try on different faces inside and pretty them all up. He says some of the women who come inside are old and should act their age, 'stead of trying to tart up like youngsters.

I can usually tell the difference between a man coming out from the store and a woman. The sound their shoes make is different. If they are alone they are always in a hurry and the women usually smell of more than one perfume at once.

When it's raining and there's not enough taxis lined up, they'll listen to us singing and sometimes get interested, though as Lewis tells it, they never look directly at us. They look away or sideways-like, until they see we're blind. Sometimes, he says he can see a smile on their face or perhaps the distant remembering of some hymn we're singing in their childhood. Then I hear them approach and place some coins or a neatly folded bill into my cup.

Lewis always helps me before he leaves at four. He takes all the bills I hand him from my cup and flattens out the ones, folds the fives in half and the tens into quarters if we get any — we sometimes do, especially at Christmas. Sometimes we even get a twenty which he hands me separately and I put it in my inside coat pocket. Once we got a hundred dollar bill. I didn't even know it until Lewis told me. He had to get change inside so Virginia and I could each have our half.

Lewis has always been good to us. He even gives us something from the store each Christmas time, like a box of fancy soaps or once he gave us each a nice woolen scarf. I keep mine nice for my daughter, Anna.

Virginia doesn't have a cup, because she must play the chords and melody on the accordion with both hands. Before the nice man from Spain gave her his old accordion, she kept forgetting to hold her cup away from her body. I can't blame her though 'cause all she had was a chipped coffee mug that was too heavy to hold out all day long. I use an old tin measuring cup that Aldo gave me at the restaurant where we sometimes eat. It weighs nothing. People don't like to get too near buskers so it's important to remember you have to reach out to them.

You never heard that word "busker?" An elderly gentleman, who used to walk by us every day with his little dog, stopped one day and asked us about a song we were singing — it was "The Royal Telephone to Jesus." He didn't know the song, but was curious to know where it came from. He was a nice man and always put a dollar or two in my cup. He had an accent like he was from away, maybe London, England, or some such place.

He asked how long we had been begging on the street. I corrected him politely, as I could tell from his voice he meant well and didn't understand our work until I explained to him that we work for our living just like he does — though I suspect he's retired or rich because he walks by us every afternoon when most folks are working.

I explained to him that we work for a living and have never begged in our lives. He said he appreciated my explaining this to him and that we provide an important service in a big city. I can sing for eight hours and never repeat a song. I know over a hundred songs by heart and Virginia knows most of them, as we've been singing together for over twenty years.

He laughed and said that he didn't mean to offend. He explained to me that where he came from we were called "buskers." I liked the sound of the word, so when people ask us what we do, I tell them we're buskers, just like the nice man said.

Everyday afterwards, he would ask us how his favorite buskers were doing. If we're in the middle of a song or hymn, he waits with his little dog to ask after us.

One day, I brought his little dog a bone that Wilson gave me from the restaurant. The dog was very happy, but I am not sure that the man was, as I heard him several yards down the street trying to wrestle the bone away from his dog which was yipping furiously at him. I "sowed dissension," as our minister used to say in Kansas. This made Ginger and me laugh for days, though Ginger doesn't laugh as much as I do. It takes a lot to make her laugh. She's seen darker days, though she doesn't carry on about it. Virginia's not much of a talker like me.

Anyway, that's why I don't like the Lighthouse. They always thought that we was beggars or *mendicants* as they'd call it. But we work for a living like most people and have a roof over our heads and eat three times a day, though I'm not quite sure that's all true for Virginia. Virginia is very secretive about where she lives and I worry that she doesn't have access to a bath, as she often smells bad, which is not good for our business.

I am not crippled, but I do sit on a folding chair. Our working day is too long for me and Virginia to stand for that much time. Virginia has a small folding stool she sits on. She is smaller than I am. I sit in a light chair like we have in our church in Brooklyn that I found on the sidewalk in front of my apartment some years back when I ran smack into it. It was large trash pickup day when people leave their furniture and refrigerators on the street for haulin' and Virginia and I have to be extra careful. It's the first Monday of every month. I felt the chair all over. It seemed in good condition and the seat felt clean to my hand so I took it up the elevator to my apartment and washed it thoroughly with a sponge and some hand soap.

I call it my apartment, but it's really just a room. There is a small corner sink and one of those half-pint refrigerators that fits underneath. My bed is against the far wall and I have nice shelves for clothes and dolls and things. It's small, but I count myself lucky to have it. The bathroom is down the hall. There is a big old bathtub and shower and a place to do your duty. It's usually clean when I first use it in the morning, but it's not so clean at night. I trained myself to use it before the other tenants get up.

There's lot of old men in my building and either they're all blind like me or they drink a lot and can't seem to aim their business in the toilet so by nighttime that bathroom is a mess and I don't use it at night. If I have to, I bring in some cleaning stuff and clean it myself first.

One day, I asked Eddy, whose barber shop is next door to my street entrance to keep his eye out for a big easy chair in good condition on large pickup-day and, a few weeks later when I came home from work and was fumbling for my door key coming down the corridor from the elevator, I stumbled into a large object right in front of my door. It was a big overstuffed chair with nice fake leather covering. It didn't lean back, but it had no rips or tears in it.

I walked right into it because I usually fold up my stick in the elevator since I know where my apartment is from memory — I've lived there almost 20 years — and there's never anything in the hallway.

Anyway, I got the chair in by myself by turning it on its side and pushing its top through the doorway and then bending it so the rest could get through. I set it upright over near my one window so I could pretend to look out at the passersby below.

I love that chair even more than my old bed. My bed's really just a cot now and sags in the middle. 'Course I'm a heavyset woman. My chair doesn't sag though at all, even though I spend several hours a day in it.

I usually eat my supper sitting in that chair and am extra careful not to spill any of my evening supper. I want to keep the chair nice for my daughter who sometimes sits in it when I'm working. She likes to read too, but she doesn't need Braille books, as she's sighted.

I taught her to read the Old Testament. She loves the stories 'cause I used to read them to her when she was little. She lives in a nice building nearby with a doorman and all. She has a nice job too, where they respect her. Her name is Anna.

Let me see, when did I first meet David? I think it was in January two years ago. It had been snowing for several days and Virginia and I promised ourselves we would just keep at it even though we had each saved up somewhat from the Christmas season.

Only a few times do we ever hear the same voice again other than Lewis and Officer Clemens and the old gentleman who walks his dog, though I think he goes away in the worst months of winter, as he doesn't come by for a number of weeks after Christmas.

Anyway, blind people never forget voices and this young man who asked us about some songs during one of our breaks and put a five dollar bill in my cup, came back the following day. I asked him if he lived near Bloomingdale's and he said he was visiting his grandmother in the city. He must've liked our songs because he came to hear us a number of times during that week.

The third day he asked me about "You'd Better Dig Deeper," a song we sing a lot. I learned it when I was at that home for unwed mothers in Topeka. An itinerant minister used to come every few weeks on Sunday and he would make us all sing this song. I guess he thought we had been having "carnal spells" or we wouldn't be there.

Believe me I hadn't had any "carnal spells" when I got with child at fifteen even though they all agreed it was my fault.

Virginia and I usually never repeat a song in the same day, but he wanted to hear it again so we sang it for him.

If you're having carnal spells, oh Christian brother
If you're daily doing things that you regret
The Old Man within your heart will always bother
You had better dig a little deeper yet

You had better dig deeper, you had better dig deeper
You had better dig a little deeper yet
The Old Man will always bother
And He's one you cannot smother
You had better dig a little deeper yet

If you're grouchy, cross, or pouty oh, be careful
'Tis so easy all your goodness to upset
If it's hard to keep an attitude that's prayerful
You had better dig a little deeper yet

You had better dig deeper, you had better dig deeper
You had better dig a little deeper yet
If you're grouchy, oh, be careful
It is better to be prayerful
You had better dig a little deeper yet

If you're touchy and so easily offended
If you're offish when you cannot be the pet
If your willpow'r is so strong it can't be bended
You had better dig a little deeper yet

You had better dig deeper, you had better dig deeper
You had better dig a little deeper yet
If you're easily offended
Or your will cannot be bended
You had better dig a little deeper yet

If you talk about your kinfolks or your neighbors
That old sin that does so easily beset
If you criticize your pastor and the members
You had better dig a little deeper yet

You had better dig deeper, you had better dig deeper
You had better dig a little deeper yet

If you talk about your neighbors
Or the pastor and the members
You had better dig a little deeper yet

If you have a bitter, unforgiving spirit
If you brood and ponder things you should forget
You will find there's hatred lurking very near it
You had better dig a little deeper yet

You had better dig deeper, you had better dig deeper
You had better dig a little deeper yet
'Less you've everyone forgiven
You can never go to heaven
You had better dig a little deeper yet

You'll be happy when you reach the firm foundation
And your feet upon the solid rock are set
There is wondrous peace and joy in this salvation
You had better dig a little deeper yet

David seemed to enjoy the song and I could hear him taking notes. He also asked if there were other songs that the minister taught us and we sang "Telephone to Glory" for him.

Central's never "busy," always on the line;
You may hear from Heaven almost any time;
'Tis a royal service, free for one and all;
When you get in trouble, give this royal line a call.

Refrain

Telephone to glory, O what joy divine!

I can feel the current moving on the line,
Built by God the Father for His loved and own,
We may talk to Jesus thru this royal telephone.

There will be no charges, telephone is free,
It was built for service, just for you and me;
There will be no waiting on this royal line,
Telephone to glory always answers just in time.

Refrain

Fail to get the answer, Satan's crossed your wire,
By some strong delusion, or some base desire;
Take away obstructions, God is on the throne,
And you'll get your answer thru this royal telephone.

Refrain

If your line is "grounded," and connection true
Has been lost with Jesus, tell you what to do;
Prayer and faith and promise, mend the broken wire,
'Till your soul is burning with the Pentecostal fire.

Refrain

Carnal combinations cannot get control
Of this line to glory, anchored in the soul;
Storm and trial cannot disconnect the line,
Held in constant keeping by the Father's hand divine.

The minister who visited the home wasn't a very nice man. My roommate Millie described him as "flinty," which to me sounds like hard stone. He had a high squeaky voice and often seemed to be discomposed when he sermoned us or tried to teach us one of his preaching songs.

I grew to dislike his visits and, one time, didn't show up for his Sunday preaching. But the mistress sent Millie for me and Millie told me I had to go or lose my Sunday treat for two weeks. Sunday treats were always fresh, ripe fruit and I so loved the taste of the oranges, pears, and watermelon that we got special on Sunday afternoon. I scurried off behind Millie and made up some excuse for why I hadn't come.

Millie and I thought that he was the kind of preacher who came late to the Lord and had done a lot of bad things before he found Jesus. The bad ways were still in his voice and neither of us thought he had the gentleness of a lamb in Jesus' flock. We girls all remained suspicious of him. Millie described his craggy, pinched face to me like a wrinkled prune, but I had never seen a prune before so I could not conjure an image of him.

His scratchy, high-pitched voice told me all I needed to know about him, though. His songs were all about carnal combinations. I think he was obsessed by them. Maybe it's why he chose our school for his sermonizing. He stopped coming after a few months and I felt much better for his leaving.

David asked me the other day if he could talk to me more after I got off work. Normally, I don't like to fraternize or tell people where I live. There are still crazy people in the world and, apart from Lewis, Aldo, Eddy, and a few others, I don't seek out the company of men. There's lots of men in my building who are unsavory as my bible school teacher used to say. That is they won't work or they take drugs or use women badly or live in a bottle. I mind my own business and nobody bothers a fat, old blind lady.

David seemed different though. He was shy and asked lots of questions about our songs. You can tell if someone is sincere like David or just evading and has another thing under mind. Virginia liked him after a bit and said so, and Virginia's distrusting of most folks. She keeps to herself and barely acknowledges Lewis who is so kind to us and once even fixed the hinge on her accordion case for her.

Anyway, I told David where I lived and told him he could come visit me the following Monday afternoon. We take Monday off and sing the other six days to make ends meet. At Christmas we usually sing every day, as people are more giving at Christmas and there's more folks on the street. It's the one time of year where they think about kin and other folks and not so much about their own selves and what they want or need.

I heard a knock on the door and got up out of my comfy chair. I have a Fox lock on my door and it takes me a minute to get it undone with my key.

Once inside, I invited David to sit in my chair, but he offered to sit on my bed and I sat back down.

Without any beating around the bush, he asked me if he could record Virginia and me singing. He said that our songs were important and that there were many he had never heard. He said he was an amateur folklorist — I think I have that word right. He was interested in our songs and where they come from. He asked if I knew the stories behind the songs and I said that I had learned them in different homes that I had been placed in and also in churches. Ginger had taught me a few songs as well. She was from Missouri and Kansas too, but had grown up with different traditions from me.

David's a polite boy. I'm not used to young men being polite and showing me respect. I liked that about him right away. He must have been raised in a family where his folks taught him respect for his elders. I offered him some tea. I don't drink coffee and he offered to get it, but it's better if I do it. You see my hot plate can be cranky and if the cord isn't just so, it spits and sputters and won't heat up. I didn't offer him milk in his tea. I don't keep milk here anymore. It spoils before I can drink it 'cause I only drink it in my tea. Aldo gave me a bag of milk powder that acts like real milk though it doesn't taste like it. It takes the harshness out of the tea. I also use sugar. David had his tea black. I put the bag in his cup before I put it in mine so his would have more flavor. I don't like strong tea anyway.

David asked me where I came from like he knew I wasn't city folk. I told him I was born in Missouri. He asked me if I was blind from birth or if I'd ever been sighted. I didn't want him pitying me so at first I didn't tell him how I got blinded. I felt comfortable with David though and later told him. He was interested in me and didn't seem to want nothing for it.

I don't tell the story for pity. It's just a fact. Lots of men, and women too, can't control their desire for drink and I suppose that was true of the doctor who came to the house to help my mother bring me into this world. I only know the story from my grandmother Hoover who was always kind to me even after my father left me up for adoption. She told me the story during the short time I was with her before I went to the St. Louis School for the Blind.

Well, I was born in a little town in Missouri called Puxico. It's between Poplar Bluff and Advance. I was born in either 1916 or 1915 and, somewhere or other, since my parents died very early, it was lost track of. My mother died when I was a year and half old and my father, when I was eight. I asked my father one time how old I was and he says, "Oh, seven or eight," and, you know, he didn't know.

My father's name was David Elmer Hoover and my mother's name was Cora. I don't know what her middle name was. Her maiden name was Parks. And I had a half-sister by my mother and then later on when my father married again, after my mother died, I had a half-sister by that marriage and a step-sister. My stepmother had a child before she married my father; then also my Daddy had a child before he married my mother. It was a mix-up, lots of halves, no wholes. So I was the only child of the second marriage for both my father and my mother.

Mother was bleeding extra heavy and my father was drinking and at a loss as to what to do. My mother must have told him to get the doctor. We had no phone so he had to beg a ride with the neighbors who didn't have a phone either. He arrived several hours later with the local doctor. The doctor did what he had to do to stop my mother bleeding. He pulled me out, slapped my bottom and washed my eyes out with boric acid, but it wasn't boric acid like they use to clean out a baby's eyes. You see sex diseases were rampant in those days and baby's eyes often got infected in the birth canal, so they always rinsed the baby's eyes out with a solution of boric acid. The doctor, like my father, had been drinking and got the wrong vial of acid out of his case and blinded me.

My father didn't take notice and my mother had passed out. He told my father only that I was blind from birth, expressed his condolences, and left without asking for payment.

I found this out later only 'cause the doctor found Jesus and confessed the story to a local minister who, in turn, told me when he drove me down to the Baptist Home. I had always thought I was born blind until then.

I don't bear him any ill will, though I wish I had never heard the story. I would rather believe that I was born blind than to know that, for a few minutes at least, I could see the world before I was too young to take any of it in.

I'm not usually a talker, but David seemed to like to hear my tellin' and I wasn't sure I had ever told it to anyone before. Virginia has never been much interested in my past, though I have often asked her about hers. Virginia's words are short and sometimes harsh to the ear, like she doesn't like tellin' her story but we been together so long she'll usually answer a question if I ask her. Unlike me, Virginia was blind from birth and doesn't talk much about her time before going to live with her grandfather and then later to the Home for the Blind. She can recall her kinfolk but don't seem to like to talk much about her growing-up years.

I don't remember so much about my own parents either. I think I can remember the sound of my mother's voice, but now I can't be sure what's memory and what's yearnin'.

My mother died when I was eighteen months. She had pneumonia and shortly after, she died. Why, my father just up and married again and I went to live with this stepmother. From there they sent me as a day student to the St. Louis School for the Blind. I started when I was four and then, when I was eight, my father died.

Well, I first started with music in the St. Louis School for the Blind. I had a friend her name was Annie Laura Richards, and we had a big, long built-in.... We called it the cloister. It was a big porch that was built in, and we'd walk up and down this porch, and, of course, we could have it either winter, spring or fall 'cause it was built in, and we'd walk up and down this cloister and we'd sing songs together. She took the alto part and I'd take the soprano part.

We'd pick up little songs, now I don't know where we'd learn the words to the songs — to some of the songs that we knew. We wouldn't know a whole song 'cause we had absolutely no way of knowing the words for it. I mean we'd just pick up little snatches of what we'd hear and we'd.... Oh, we had about twelve, fourteen little pieces of songs that we'd sing, and, of course, Annie could play the piano a little bit, but, course, I couldn't.

I started taking piano lessons when I was about eight, but I had absolutely no talent for the piano. And, of course, we'd read in Braille and'd have to memorize one hand while we played it, then we'd have to read with the other hand while we memorized the part for the other hand. So we'd have to completely memorize our whole piece before we could really put it together and play it.

After my father died, I had a great uncle, at least that's what he called himself. He was 58 and he started messin' with me in ways that he shouldn't. Oh, he'd get all religious and explain how he should "check me out" in places where no man should check a little girl out.

He'd make up long elaborate stories about how it was the Lord's will and right and all and it was only for my own good and that he was tryin' to help me so I wouldn't get in trouble. Then he got more threatenin' and I got scared and told.

Well, then I was moved to Kansas because I had a grandmother there — that is, well, I was gonna be nine in November and my father died in October, and so then for the summer, I went to live with this grandmother in Kansas, the oil fields. So then I kept going to the St. Louis School for the Blind for a couple of years more because my Grandmother Hoover was my guardian over some money my Dad had left me from his life insurance, about twelve hundred dollars; but my stepmother she got her hold on it and spent most of it and Grannie Hoover took her to court to get it away from her but there wasn't much left. Since my Grandmother Hoover lived in Missouri, why I was still entitled to go to the St. Louis School for the Blind, but then, when I was eleven, I started going to the

Kansas City School for the Blind and, of course, it was there that I first met Virginia Brown.

How we really happened to meet was... Course, I was eleven, but I was gonna be twelve in November, so they were all giving me a birthday spanking. They were kinda giving me initiation. You know in the schools lot of times you had to have an initiation the first year, you know, 'cause they wanna see what you're made out of.

So they all had me layin' on a table and some was sittin' on my feet so I couldn't get up, and the rest of them, they'd take their turns and they'd give me a big spanking. So Virginia, she came over and she gave me a swat or two and she said, "All right now, that's enough." And she said, "Now, I'm going to have to tell the supervisor." And so, they all got off then and skun out you know. But I wouldn't have done anything 'cause I was gonna show them that I was just, you know, that I belonged there.

So when I had to go to the School for the Blind in Kansas City, towards the end of my time there, Virginia and me got to know each other better and started singing church songs together; and of course, Virginia can play the piano — she's very talented that way. And we'd sing our little church songs and we found out we could sing together. We enjoyed doing it and people enjoyed hearing it so we started singing together there in the School for the Blind. We didn't do a whole lot of it, but that's where we got our start.

But here I go rushin' ahead of the story again. Slow down, Baybie, slow down....

My grandmother was a war widow. Her husband died in what she called "The Great War." I never knew which war that was, but even as a little girl I felt sorrow for her. She was a kindly woman and had few resources except for her widow's pension for the two of us to live on, so we lived frugal. I remember helping her with her hand wash and balancing on a wooden fruit crate to help her hang out the wash. We lived in a small tenement outside of Kansas City. I forget the name of the town, but it was small enough so neighbors sometimes came by and asked after us. I liked living there. My grandmother didn't treat me like a cripple. She always said the world was a hard place and I would have to be strong, even as a girl, to cope with it. She made me feel important even though I was blind and a girl.

When I switched to the Kansas City School for the Blind, which was a live-in school in Kansas City. I didn't want to go and the day they came for me, I cried and carried on, kicking and screaming. So finally, one of the men just picked me up and threw me over his shoulder and tossed me into the backseat of a car with my small valise of clothes and a doll and drove off. It was the last time I ever saw my grandmother, and I don't know whatever became of her. I guess I was an orphan after that. It was the first time I ever remember being angry and afraid at the same time. My grandmother had told me to behave and be strong. Even so, I put up a terrible fuss.

It took a long time before I adapted to life at the School. My roommate was a girl named Anna Durwood. She was nice and we liked each other immediately. She told me she'd come there from the almshouse where she lived with her mother who'd died of the fever. She was very shy and had long hair almost down to her waist. Us blind kids would feel each other's faces with our fingers to see what we looked like. Not everyone's comfortable being touched all over like that and you have to ask.

We had to share a bed as the school was overcrowded and I remember the first night snuggling in bed together and touching each other all over to see what we looked like. Anna had only recently lost her sight from a bacteria disease that was quite common in those days. She said the almshouse had lots of disease and sickness and had only one doctor who came there twice a week. I don't know where it was, but most poor folks she said'd rather live on the street than go to the almshouse. Her mother tried to make a go of it basting shirts and ironing in their second story apartment for a local tailor, but finally had to sell her sad iron to make rent.

Anna'd only been blind for a year. Her memory of things in the world became my library and we would lie in bed at night after lights were turned out at 8:30 and she'd tell about things I'd never seen. She told me her eyes were blue and her long hair was light brown. Course brown and blue didn't have any meaning for me. She also told me that she had a birthmark on her chin that I couldn't see with my hands 'cause it was only a color. When she was little, she told me that she'd tried every night to wash the birthmark away with harsh lye soap, but that it was always still there when she dried her face and looked in the mirror. For a long time it made her cry 'cause the other kids made fun of it and called her fruity-face. She said it was strawberry red. I could taste the strawberries and conjure their feel and shape, but I couldn't see the red. I had heard people tell of all these colors before, but the words she used to describe the colors to me all involved more colors or things I'd never seen.

I loved to run my fingers through her long hair. It felt so soft and beautiful. She had no curls that I could feel. My hair was always bobbed short 'cause we had had a run of lice at my Grannie's that no amount of kerosene could rid me of. I hated it when she cut my hair short and rubbed kerosene into what little hair I had left. The boy at the corner store knew too and he'd call me boy-names and could smell the kerosene on me. I lived with that smell until I came here. It still makes me gag when I smell a kerosene lamp or stove.

Anna and I was the same age so we could do everything together and that gave us both comfort 'cause we was scared with no parents. We became like sisters and when my little girl was born I named her Anna after my first real friend.

The school was very strict and there was a routine we had to follow, but most of the lady teachers there were nice when things went hard on us. They was strict but if they saw we was sad or scared, they'd tender us a bit.

Anna had learned when she was sighted to thread a needle and to sew things. She had a needle and thread and in the rest periods she taught me how to thread a needle and how to stitch a seam. What patience that girl had. I never had a kin or friend with such patience for my fumbling. Some blind people never can thread a needle. My first sewed seams made her laugh out loud. She said they looked like coon tracks from what her fingers could feel on the muslin cloth. They was all over the place but I soon earned to sew a straight seam even before I took the sewing class at school.

Sitting on our bed once, I was sewing a torn hem on my nightshirt and I dropped the needle. I was so scared 'cause I knew it was Anna's only needle. I felt everywhere for it and fretted over how I would tell her if I couldn't find it. I found it that night in bed when I rolled over, "right where the sun don't shine" as my Grannie used to say. I put it back in her sewing case the next morning and told her the story the following night. Oh, how we did laugh.

I think back often about that school and mostly about Anna. I mix up my memories of her and my memories of my own daughter sometimes.

When it came time to go to the school, my grandmother began to treat me different. Maybe she knew I'd put up a fuss, maybe she just knew the ways of the world, but she began acting different, treating me like I wasn't her own, almost like I was a boarder.

She'd always tucked me in bed, told me a story, and kissed me goodnight after doing her lice check. We had no books but she remembered stories from her own mother's telling. Toward the end though, she would just send me to bed with no goodnight kiss or story. I couldn't understand her sudden coldness, but now, looking back on it, I can see why she did it. I recall her last story, telling me how she'd harden-off a tender shoot before planting it in the garden. She'd take down her little tomato starts from the window sill and shake them out of their tin can starter pots. She'd lay them all out on a damp cloth and carry them out to her kitchen garden where she'd dig a hole with her hands and tamp them in among the other plants growing there. "They're on their own now," she'd say, and she'd tell how the little plants would wilt and droop and complain about their new home. Then, she said, after a few days they'd buck up and begin to grow tall and straight, and then in the end of July, how they'd be heavy with red tomatoes swollen with juice and so good to eat with salt and pepper and apple vinegar.

The rising bell rang at six except on Sundays when it was seven. We'd gather in the girls' room to wash up, get dressed in our jumpers, and then go to breakfast at 6:30. We had chapel at 7:30 and our first class at 8. The morning was classes like in a real school and the afternoon was vocational classes for blind people. Anna and I took pretty much the same classes the year we started. We took raised point or what they now call

Braille, spelling, arithmetic, and grammar. I felt so dumb in those early classes and Anna would sit next to me and help me with my lessons. We were encouraged to help one another in the early classes, not like in later years when some teachers thought you was cheating. I learned slowly, but having Anna as a friend made me want to learn so I could be like her. In the afternoon was more fun and I took to it better. We had recreation, music classes, and us young'uns had some junior crafting classes like sewing, beadwork, and broom-making. I loved doing things with my hands, but we had to be careful not to get calluses or we'd have trouble reading dots. There was pumice stones in the bathrooms for the older students to use who worked a lot with their hands.

We were graded on deportment and posture too. Anna and I always got good grades there except once when we got giggling so hard in class that we were sent to the mistress' office for a talking to. I can't remember what we got laughing on, but I can remember the sound of her laughter like it was yesterday... reminds me of my daughter's laugh.

I wanted to play cornet, but there wasn't enough instruments to go around so I studied harmony and singing. The teacher, Miss Lula, said I had a good singing voice and good pitch for harmonizing so that's where my singing career began, I would say.

Late in the afternoon, we'd have recreation which was mostly walking in pairs around the grounds and taking turns on the three swing sets. Older kids got to do more things like running, broad jumping, and rope climbing but always under the watchful eye of Mr. Tubbs, the rec. supervisor.

The hour before dinner we'd have to ourselves but had to be in our rooms. After dinner, we grouped up by age and teachers would read us stories from books that were approved by the mistress for our age group. I 'specially loved the reading hour. Anna and I would sit on the assembly room floor and hold hands. Little comforts like holding hands were indulged with the youngest of us. Lights out was at nine and bed check at 9:30. I think most kids were like Anna and me, whispering late into the night about the day's activities, what we'd learned, and what we thought or imagined up about our teachers and their lives outside the school.

The scariest memory for me was the fire drills we had four times a year. No matter how many times they explained 'em to us, I'd get so anxious I'd forget what we was supposed to do when the big bell rang. We called it the "big bell" 'cause it was different from the one they rang for changing classes and marking activity periods. It was deeper and louder than the class bell. Two times a year they ran the fire drills in the middle of the night and that's what scared me most 'cause we never knew whether or not they was drills or a real fire.

My grandmother had told me once about an uncle I'd never heard tell of that died in a barn fire when he was only ten. His father — what would have been my grandfather — though I never knew many of my kin, had sent him in to finish forking the loose hay to the back of the hay loft. The hay underneath had been stowed wet and a fire had been brewing down under the hay he was forking for several days. The way she told it all the hay dust from his forking exploded like gas and he was burnt alive in the fire. Then it spread from the barn to the house nearby, but my grandmother escaped from the house, but lost all her clothes and personals.

Ever since she told me that story, I been scared to death of fire and that fear stayed with me at the School for the Blind. No matter how many times Anna explained to me that the drill would save us from a fire, I would have panic when I heard that bell go off and just cry out to Anna to let me hold on to her and follow her. I could never remember the drill for leaving the building, but Anna knew and would lead me to safety the way we was supposed to go. I remember crying all the way down those endless staircases while she told me to hold on to the rail. Other kids must a been scared too, 'cause I could hear 'em whimpering and crying. We was on the third floor and it was a long way to the rec. field where we was supposed to congregate and be counted before the bell rang again twice and we could return to our rooms. I'd keep asking Anna, "You sure there's no fire? How do they know for sure?" I knew that boy-uncle had no way of knowing there was a fire smoldering underneath where he was working neither.

Our room was nice. Some rooms had two beds and four girls living in them. Anna and me had one of the small rooms on the third floor. It was only twice as wide as the bed, but it was plenty comfort for us two. We was small girls. The bed was warm. The wire-bottom beds sagged in the middle so we was always bunched together. The mattresses were stuffed with wool batting and heavy and we had to turn our mattresses, make our beds, and change our own linen. The older girls helped with the washing every Saturday. If we needed help, the house matron would help us or show us how to do a chore. Folks was patient on account of our being blind and took the time to show us how to do things. We had to sweep out our rooms on Saturday with brooms made by the older girls in broom-making class and change our own clothes as well. We each kept two sets of under-things, a cotton jumper, and a cambric nightshirt.

My favorite thing of the week was the Saturday evening bath after supper. The floor matron would fill the tub half-up with warm water and we girls would take turns in pairs bathing, starting at the end of the hall and moving down the corridor. We'd line up in our nightshirts with one of us holding our towel that we shared — there was one towel per room. When it came our turn we could tell 'cause the girls next door to us would be leaving the bathroom and that would signal for us to go in, strip down and hop into the warm soapy water. The water was changed after every six pairs of us had bathed and we each got ten minutes in the tub. The matron was a kindly soul and oversaw us washing ourselves to make sure we washed everywhere. She would then check us for head lice. Anna and I would take turns washing each other's backs and then we'd lie back on the warm porcelain and just enjoy the luxury. If the water cooled off, the matron would add some hot water so it was always warm even for the last girls.

Meals was good, better'n we'd had at home. Some of the girls was orphans like Anna. I'd never thought about it, but maybe I was an orphan with no mother or father. I never did figure if having a grandmother meant you wasn't an orphan. Anna said I wasn't an orphan 'cause I'd had a kindly grandmother. Anyway we appreciated knowing there'd be three meals every day.

The meals was the same for each day of the week. The mistress or a house matron would always say a prayer to Jesus first. We sat at long tables, twenty girls to a table. Table manners was very important and they'd watch over us 'cause our table manners was a big part of our deportment grade and that was as important as any other grade we got. Spilling food on the oilcloth table cover would count against your grade.

Breakfast was almost always hot cereal and milk and sugar, except Sunday when we had flapjacks with butter and powdered sugar and sometimes bacon. Once the cook must have gotten some raisins and put them in the oatmeal as a surprise. Some of the girls thought they was roaches or flies or something until the flavor of them burst onto their tongues and then they wanted them all the time but I don't remember ever having them again. Cookie must have gotten some special.

The food at lunch was different each day. That was the meal where we ate meat and vegetables. Some of the girls didn't like vegetables, but Anna and I did, 'specially peas and carrots. Sometimes when there was no meat, we'd get baked beans cooked in brown sugar and molasses with fatback. That was one of our favorites.

We always had bread at lunch and dinner and we was expected to use a slice of the bread to find our food and to use it as a backstop so we didn't spill food off the plate when we forked it up. Anna and me used to call that slice our "dustpan," and our fork would be the "whiskbroom" like we swept up our rooms with. Worn sheets was torn up into strips that were used as cloth table napkins so we'd learn how to eat proper and sit at a table with sighted folks and not look different than they was.

Supper was often just some bread with left over lunchmeat on it or butter or pork lard spread with sugar. Sunday was the only day we had dessert, usually baked pies with whatever fruit was in the root cellar. That was the biggest treat. In the winter when there was no fruit except stored apples, Cookie'd sometimes make up sugar pies that was so sweet. Oh, we loved that pie. Don't think there was anything in it but brown sugar, butter, and Karo syrup. I never did learn to cook so I can't tell. Some of the older girls worked in the kitchen helping prepare food, washing and drying dishes and such. If you're blind, you have to be extra careful around knives and sharp things so you had to be taught to work in there. I never did, even as much as I came to like food. Later I worked in the laundry.

Oh, and yes, there was boys there, but we hardly ever heard them 'cept at Sunday services and in another part of the rec. field hootin' and hollerin'. We was kept apart almost all the time. Anna and I was just as happy about that as we had never met any boys that was nice to us, course they was mostly sighted and in those days, it was a shame to be blind and we'd get teased for it.

Time passed slowly at the School for the Blind, perhaps 'cause Anna and me liked it so much and liked each other. We kept company for three years there until we was almost fourteen. In seventh grade, we was evaluated and counseled about what we was going to be when we growed up. We later found out that counseling determined our future in the school. The school was practical about blind folk and knew that life wouldn't be easy for most of us, 'cause few of us came from well-to-do families or any family at all that would take us in and provide for us. So the school authorities'd decide about our crafting and how we would make a living. I told that I wanted to be a singer in a choir. The vocation person told me that singing was not a way to make a living and there wasn't any blind singers what ever became famous and got rich, much less made a living. She said I could have a practical vocation, earn my keep, and sing in the church choir on

Sunday, but that kinda singing wouldn't pay my keep.

I'd learned some sewing and washing, but that wasn't enough and a decision was made to foster me out to a farmin' family. I asked if Anna could come with me and they evaded my question by saying that would depend on her own counsellin'. I could always tell when someone was evading in the tone of their voice... still can to this day.

As it worked out, she was to be fostered out too, but to a different family so that's how we came to know we was gonna be separated. We thought we was sisters and we'd heard tell that family wasn't separated, that every efforts was made to keep brothers and sisters together when they left the school to go to a foster family or to a trade.

The richer kids whose families could pay tuition got to stay on through high school and get higher learnin' and fix on one trade so they could make a go of it when they returned to their families. I guess we wasn't so lucky. Plus we didn't have any money or kinfolk. My grandmother had told me when I left that she wasn't going to write 'cause she didn't want me to be homesick and that I would more easily accept being there, but I 'spect she simply never learned to write letters. In one sense, I was luckier than she was, 'cause I could write and read raised point pretty well at twelve.

Course, they was wrong about me earning a living singing. That's what I done all my life. It ain't easy work, but it's work and it sometimes even pays good. I got enough to eat, a warm place to sleep, and a beautiful daughter who reminds me of Anna.

I'm a sojourner, always have been a sojourner, Now I 'spect you know what a sojourner is but I'll tell ya anyway. Anna and me sojourned at The School for the Blind. My next sojourn started off in sadness at the loss of my only true friend Anna, but for the first while was good enough. At fifteen, I was fostered out to the Desmets family what had a small farm near Bazine, Kansas. I'd hadn't ever heard of Bazine, but it was farming country and far from the school. When I was readyin' to leave, the mistress of the school brought in a carpetbag valise with a metal snap and some used clothes from her church. I tried on some and the ones that fit she packed carefully. The clothes smelled like carbolic. I got to keep my underthings and nightshirt, but had to give up my jumper. I'd been through three jumpers in my five years at the school. Each was used and they always gave you one bigger than what fit you proper so you could grow into it. That way they lasted longer on one girl. There was also a pair of lace-up shoes that was a little too big, but that I could wear well enough. We never wanted for socks as many of the older girls knitted socks for the school and that was the clothes we wore out the fastest. The mistress packed me two pairs of nice wool socks.

I was starting to grow a bosom earlier than most girls. Anna didn't have any signs yet, but we didn't have brassieres or any such things so I didn't ask. We hadn't learned much about growing up and body changing. Anna and me heard from the older girls that there's no class on it, but the mistress does have a talk with girls individually when they begin to show woman signs. We heard from the older girls lots about monthlies and how they was supposed to be managed but mine hadn't begun yet nor had Anna's, but we talked about it some together.

I felt like I was dyin' when it came time to leave. Anna was leaving to go to a family somewhere in Missouri a few weeks after me so it was my parting when we had to make our goodbyes. I can't tell you how sad I was. I didn't put on no fuss like I had when the man carried me out of my grandmother's house. I just cried and cried. Anna and I would hold each other. The last night we slept in our bed, we stayed up all night carrying on about how we'd find each other again and maybe live and work together. We joked that between us we was a whole person and knew how to do a lot of useful things. I knew I'd miss her memory of being sighted.

When it came time for me to be taken to the train station, I just left. I'll never forget the touch of her hand in mine or on my cheek when she was feelin' my tears or the sounds of her sobbin' voice when she said goodbye. I'm sixty-four today and I ain't never seen or heard from Anna. She was my dearest friend and I don't even know where she might be or if she's still walking on this earth or lying in it.

I'd never been on a train before. There was a note pinned to my dress saying that I was Nadine Hoover and that I was getting off in Wakeeney, Kansas, and was to be met by Elroy and Hetty Desmets at the station there.

I tried to imagine my new fosters. The mistress couldn't or wouldn't answer any of my questions about the family I was going to live with other than to say that they had been approved by the authorities as upstanding folks. They didn't have no kids and that I would be welcome as one of their own. I wasn't sure I wanted to be, as I didn't know them and I'd heard enough tales of hardship during my time in the school and from Anna from her time at the almshouse to be apprehensing about my new family.

The Negro porter was kindly and helped me off the train with my valise in Wakeeney. I stood on the platform not knowing where I was and just waiting for someone to come for me.

After a time just standing there holding my bag, I managed to find a bench up against the station and under the roof I think, 'cause I could feel it cooler out of the sun. I was scared that nobody was there to meet me and after awhile, I pretended that Anna was with me sitting on the bench and I talked to her about it.

After an hour or so, I heard my name called out from nearby. "Nadine Hoover?" I heard. I stood up and said aloud that I was Nadine Hoover. It was a woman's voice and I could hear footsteps approaching. She seemed nervous for a grownup and introduced herself saying that she was Mrs. Desmets and that the man next to her was her husband Elroy. Someone picked up my valise and a man-voice said to follow him. I knew then that they didn't know for blind people. Standing back, I asked if I might hold Mrs. Desmets' hand while we walked, and she seemed surprised at first but soon realized that I couldn't see where I was going. The platform was elevated somewhat and I needed help finding and going down the few steps to where there might be a car. We stopped and a man with calloused hands helped me into the front seat of what must have been a truck from its height and the gear shifter being in the middle near my legs.

Mrs. Desmets made polite conversation on the long drive to their farmhouse. They had no idea about being blind and seemed embarrassed to ask about it for fear of making me uncomfortable so I kinda took the lead and explained where I would need help and how I might need their patience sometimes as I was tryin' things out. I had no idea of the lay of their property and I asked if the yard was flat or hilly, if my room was on the second or the ground floor? I think they was surprised by all my questions, but it's hard for a sighted person to imagine blind tribulations. They can't imagine what they couldn't see if they was blind.

The house was small and not at all like the school. There was water to the kitchen sink but no bathroom. There was a privy some ways away from the house. I asked if they would be willing to put some stakes and a string between the house and the privy until I got used to walking the stretch. Mr. Desmets said that a string wouldn't help much in the winter but that he'd do it for now 'til I learned where it was.

Blind folk have proprioception. We learned this at school. It's like a sixth sense that tells you where things is. With no sight, the other senses tune up sharp and create like a sixth sense. I can sense someone near me even if I can't hear 'em. I knew after a few weeks living in my new home, I'd figure where things was. I did have to ask Mr. and Mrs. Desmets to tell me if they moved anything so I wouldn't break nothing by mistake. I think that the getting-used-to was harder for them than for me. You see I had plenty a practice finding my way around strange places, but I was the first blind person they'd ever encountered up close. It was strange for us both. I rely so much on the sound of a person's voice to read the air of what's happening and my new fosters was so uncomfortable that it was hard at first to understand what they was feeling about me.

Mrs. Desmets tried to be outgoing and kindly, asking a lot of question about how it was to be blind. Mr. Desmets did too at first, but soon seemed to lose patience like he thought I was taking advantage by my blindness. He wasn't around much so, Mrs. Desmets and I began to build a friendship and she came to understand my ways more quickly. I could tell she wanted me to be her daughter and I was willing to oblige, though I didn't want to be, and knew I never would be. I had already grown too much and valued my own independence. There was no one now other than Anna would ever feel like kin.

My room was up a flight of uneven stairs. The house was not as well built as the school I'd lived in for the last four years. Floor boards wasn't even everywhere 'cept in the kitchen where there was linoleum. There was a scatter rug in the living room, but it didn't lie flat so I had to be extra mindful. My bedroom was under the eave so I had to watch my head and soon got used to where the roof sloped and where the bed was placed. It was a wooden bed, sturdy enough but handmade; I could tell from the feel of the head and footboards. The mattress was filled with husks rather than batting and I could feel the husks through some of the ticking. In the summer, I just made my bed up so's the blanket was under the bottom sheet and it made my lying down smoother. There was no window to catch a breeze. They probable thought I didn't need a window 'cause I couldn't see but a blind person still likes to feel a cool breeze sometimes.

I told Mrs. Desmets that I liked chores, explaining that she might have to show me how a couple of times but that I liked helping round the house. It was late summer and she was beginnin' her canning so she'd give me green beans to pinch and string, carrots to clean and cut up just so, and them little cucumbers to wash for pickling. I had never done these things and enjoyed it very much. She told me I was helpful and that felt good. She asked me about my kin and, I suspect, expected a long conversation, but there wasn't much for me to say. Not having known my mother and father. I told her 'bout my kindly grandmother, but allowed that I didn't know if she was alive. I think she thought I was keepin' something from her, but there just wasn't more to tell.

I loved the smell and touch of all the raw gardened things and thought that cannin' was fun. I was very careful with the paring knife and used it on a pine cutting board on the table. I don't think I made any mistakes and Mrs. Desmets seemed pleased with my helping and my company.

My other favorite thing was going to the Bethel Pentecostal Church in Bazine. On Sunday morning, we'd get as dressed as we could and head off in the truck to Sunday services. I'd always sit in the middle between Mr. and Mrs. Desmets 'cause of the gear shifter. I didn't like having it between my legs 'cause Mr. Desmets was always grabbing it and shiftin it up and down and his rough hand would sometimes rub on me there. I didn't like being touched by anyone but Anna, but especially not by men.

I could sometimes feel what the two was wearing to church. Mrs. Desmets wore a cotton dress like always, but it smelled of starch 'cause I know she ironed it regular. I liked to imagine it all covered with flowery pictures or maybe horses. Mr. Desmets wore a scratchy suit that felt like woolen winter pants. I would try to sit as far away as I could from him, but I could feel the upper sleeve of his coat on my bare upper arms.

There was a lot to hear at church, singin', preachin', and sometimes talkin' in tongues, which I'd never heard before, fast-talking, voice risin' and fallin' about the spirit coming into their souls and describing the feelings and all, and how the Holy Spirit would enter the person at Baptism and take all their sins away and lead them into the light of the Lord, which I could imagine for myself.

On my fifth Sunday there, I was baptized because I couldn't remember for the preacher if I'd been baptized before or not. He allowed that one could never be baptized enough in the Holy Spirit and so I was baptized one Sunday in the small creek not far from the church.

I most loved the singing, and that's where I learned so many of the songs I sing today, was in that little church. I asked Mrs. Desmets if I could ask the preacher if I could try out for the choir and she said yes, but Mr. Desmets said no 'cause he wasn't going to drive me to no choir practices, especially with gas up to $.12 a gallon. I so wanted to sing in that choir, but I had to satisfy myself with just listening and memorizing the words and melodies cause it was too far to walk.

They must have sung a hundred different hymns. When the choir was singing alone, I'd sing along in my mind. When the whole congregation was singing, I'd sing along as loud as I could and I think the preacher took notice 'cause after one service he complimented me on my voice.

I also wanted to stay after for Bible School and meet other kids, but Mr. Desmets was always in a hurry to get home and get back to his chores. He was one to work on Sunday like the Lord says not to, but I never thought he cottoned much to what the Lord had to say. He just wanted to be seen in church by his neighbors, I figured. Some folks is like that I've learned. Churchin' on Sunday and doin' their own mind the rest of the days, only he didn't even wait 'til Monday.

I'd only heard the standard hymns at the School for the Blind in Kansas City and there wasn't no hootin', hollerin', and "praise-the-Lords" at the Lutheran Church we attended in Kansas City. It was a quiet service but the hymns were beautiful and have stayed with me to this day.

The first feel of fall came in late October and I had pretty much gotten used to things at the Desmets. Mr. Desmets spent most of his days tractoring in the fields. I could hear the engine far away coming and going as he row-cropped his fields. Mrs. Desmets soon got in the habit of describing events on the farm so I could see them in my imagination.

My favorite job was gathering the eggs in the afternoon from under Mrs. Desmets' biddies. I'd leave by the screen door in the kitchen, down two wooden steps, and onto the dirt. I could walk straight to the henhouse door and put my hand right on the hook and eye lock. I'd open the door quickly and step inside and close it again without locking it so's no chickens could get out. I'd shuffle slowly through their peckin' yard as the ground there was ever changing 'cause the hens'd scrabble around digging up stones and makin' big holes for their dirt baths so I'd have to walk careful.

Inside the henhouse, the far wall was all nesting boxes where the biddies laid their eggs. The broody ones'd stay in their nests all day warmin' their eggs. At first I was too scared to reach under them 'cause they'd put up a loud fuss and peck at my hand, but once I realized it didn't hurt, I got bolder and I'd reach in under their warm feathers and pull out their eggs. The eggs was warm to the touch. I'd then put them carefully in the pocket of my jumper, careful not to bang 'em together or to bang into anything in the henhouse. I'd usually get between four and eight eggs each day. I soon learned that the length of the daylight had a lot to do with how many eggs they laid so there was sometimes no eggs or one or two in the short days of fall. Mrs. Desmets was tryin' to get Mr. Desmets to run 'lectricity out to the henhouse so she could have a light on in there in winter 'cause that would encourage the biddies to lay more, but he never did.

One day when I was helping Mrs. Desmets with laundry chores, she asked me if I'd had the curse yet. I'd heard tell of it so I wasn't without any knowing and I told her that I didn't think so. She told me there was some spots in my underthings that indicated it was coming on and that I would have to take precautions so as not to ruin my few clothes. Her talking about this made me uncomfortable even though she tried to be comforting in her explaining.

Since I could sew, she set me cutting and sewing some old cotton rags together into pads thick enough to absorb whatever blood I might make and explained that I should put them in my underpants when the time came. I asked how I'd know since I couldn't see the spotting or feel any bleeding. She had not thought about this and said she'd consider on it.

Since I changed my underthings every week like at the school, we agreed that she'd keep an eye out for spots, and that when she saw them, I'd wear the pad of rags inside them for the following week. I wanted to see what she was talking about and didn't understand hardly anything about birthing and monthlies and all that. I'd heard joking about sex, but didn't know for it.

Our plan seemed to work and I gradually began to sense when I was having a period coming on. I figured I was becoming a woman even at fifteen since my breasts was already pretty developed and I had hair under my arms and in the other place. We was both uncomfortable talking on this, but she seemed to be trying hard to mother me even though I was fostered.

Course, I never knew what I looked like. I could touch myself all over and feel where I'd grown up and changed or if I needed a haircutting or a bathing, but I still couldn't image what I looked like.

One day at supper, I asked Mrs. Desmets if I was a pretty girl. She seemed surprised and allowed that "I was as pretty as I needed to be in this world." I didn't know what she meant by that and Mr. Desmets, who rarely said much at all to me, said, "Don't go getting ideas 'bout being pretty. You're a plain girl and that's best."

I never asked again what I looked like. Only person I knew I could trust to ask that question to was Anna. I wish she could have seen me when she was sighted so she could explain to me how I looked. She would use words from her sighted days in a way that a blind person like me could understand. I always said she was my mirror. I never will know how I look. I miss Anna terribly. Some nights I lie in bed and pretend she is there with me and we talk quietly until I fall asleep.

Days became very much the same. I missed learning and school. Other than my grandmother, I had no experience being a blind person among sighted people and didn't know what an understanding gap there was. Sighted people can't imagine what it is to be blind and, no matter how much they care, it's hard for them to adapt to having a blind person with them. Mrs. Desmets was patient and understanding, but couldn't ever conjure the tribulations of a blind person, let alone a child. Mr. Desmets didn't seem to care much. I was a chore and I guess he figured he had enough chores on the farm without adding me. He soon gave up even addressing me when he walked by, though I always showed him respect like I'd been taught and said "Good morning, Mr. Desmets" or "Good night, Mr. Desmets.

I've always been a modest person and at the School for the Blind, there was no need for modesty 'cause we girls were all together in one wing and the boys was all in another, and there was no way inside the building that boys and girls could ever be together. Also, we was all blind so spyin' on one another never occurred to anybody.

It was different though at the Desmets 'cause I was the only blind person. I was grateful they didn't have any boys. I did sometimes wish they had a girl child though, someone could be a sister like Anna had been to me. There was a big tin basin that Mrs. Desmets and I used for bathing in the kitchen. She'd fill it with warm water heated on the wood stove and she'd let me get in first, suds up with a big bar of store-bought lye soap and bathe. Then I'd dry off with a worn-smooth towel. She'd add some hot water, get in and do her bathing as well. We'd usually do this before supper well before Mr. Desmets came in from his chores.

He'd bathe outside. There was a tap right behind the iron kitchen sink on the outside of the house and he'd rinse the hay and dirt off'n himself there. He must've had a bar of soap out there, too, and then he'd rinse himself off 'cause he'd smell of lye soap when he came in. He could only do this in the summer and fall, 'cause in winter the water was too cold and there'd be snow on the ground. Then he'd begin to have his own bath on a Saturday night in the kitchen just like us. Course, he didn't need to be modest around me 'cause I couldn't see even if I'd wanted to and Mrs. Desmets, well she was his wife anyway.

I was wary from the start though and only felt safe bathing when Mrs. Desmets was around and I knew he wasn't. I'd heard girls talk about boys peeping on them before they came to school and I heard the minister preachin' about modesty.

Things seemed right enough the first year, though I missed learnin' new things. Mrs. Desmets made use of what I'd learned before I came, but didn't teach me new things unless I asked and she knew the answer. I came to understand after some time that she didn't know much about things that I wanted to learn about, and I began to hanker for my next sojourn even though I had no idea what or where it might be. I knew I wouldn't spend the rest of my life on the Desmets farm.

My troubles began after the first snowfall when the work in the fields was mostly done and there was no more to do around the farm, other than split and stack stove wood, feed the hogs and chickens and milk the two cows. It didn't seem to be much of a farm, but we didn't lack for food. I think Mr. Desmets sold mostly field crops and stuff 'cause there was no big barn full of animals. I wanted to know more about the farm, but any questions I ever did ask Mr. Desmets were short-answered and Mrs. Desmets would apologize for him, saying how hard he worked and how tired he was from his chores and she'd try and answer the question I had asked.

Mr. Desmets usually went to bed right after supper and was gone before Mrs. Desmets and I came down in the morning. He'd come back in about 6:30 for his morning coffee and breakfast and then disappear again, often without saying a word or a howdy-doo. For a long time, I just thought he didn't like me, but I then came to understand he didn't treat Mrs. Desmets much better.

All this got me thinking about love and marriage. In the Braille books we read there was stories of men and woman romancing and living happily. I couldn't recollect my own parents at all and my grandmother was a widow so I'd never experienced what they was telling about.

After dinner at the school, when teachers'd read to us about people's trials and tribulations, but about how they was kept together by carin' and love and all, I'd think on it and wish for the same for me 'cause I had yet to see it in my short life, though I would in later times.

I also missed books, being read to, and storytelling. I don't think either Mr. or Mrs. Desmets could read. There was no books in the house as far as I could tell and once when Mrs. Desmets was tradin' in town, she asked Mr. Desmets if she could buy a picture magazine that had a movie star on the cover for a quarter. He denied her sayin' "What cha want that for, iss mostly words and you can't read none of 'em."

I'd have been happy if there was even story tellin' at the dinner table, but Mrs. Desmets would say, "How did your day go, Elroy?" and Mr. Desmets would answer, "Well enough," or "Not too good," or nothing at all. I couldn't tell if he even liked being at home or with me and Mrs. Desmets. Sometimes, I'd hear sadness or maybe fear in her voice, but course I couldn't see her face. She seemed a sad enough woman and I think found some solace in my company even though I was only a young girl.

I first knew that Mr. Desmets was watchin' me when I was bathin' when I heard Mrs. Desmets whisper to him, "It ain't right." I thought I could sense he was in the kitchen.

Finally, he said, "Hell, she's just a girl, ain't no wrong in it. She's our foster young-un."

Then, 'course, I knew he was in the kitchen and that his Mrs. was protestin' him seein' me naked. The basin was too small to hide in so I just scrunched up my knees and began to cry.

Mrs. Desmets then said, "Now, see what'cha done. She's scared," whereupon I heard the door slam and Mr. Desmets go outside.

"Don't fret none child, he just wanted to finish his coffee before he went out, nothing to worry on."

And that was it.

"Is he gone?" I asked, knowing he had.

"Yes, he's finishing chores. You dry up and get your nightshirt on and ready up for bed."

"Yes, Mrs. Desmets," I answered. I never did call her "Ma" like she wanted and I didn't feel right calling her Hetty so I just kept calling her "Mrs. Desmets," which let her know that I still felt a distance between us.

At first I was scared by what happened, then I was angry, but didn't have no one to tell my anger to.

The next time it came time to bathe, I didn't say anything when Mrs. Desmets was heating the water. I took my towel and clean nightgown and made my way outside to the tap. I took my clothes off, got under the water, which was much colder than I had imagined, soaped up myself and rinsed all off, dried up and came inside in my nightie. I was freezin' and knew with winter comin' that would be the last time I could shower outdoors. Besides, I was even more exposed to Mr. Desmets out there than I was in the kitchen and Mrs. Desmets wasn't around to see what was happening.

I suppose I did it just to show my anger, but I knew it didn't do much good. Blind people is often at the good will of other people and if they ain't good, there's not much a blind person can do. Least, that's how I felt.

It happened several more times and Mrs. Desmets finally gave up feudin' him on it. She gave in to him on everything it seemed and always seemed a little afraid of him. Course, I wasn't around for all their discussin', but I knew I wouldn't be scared of no kin, but then he wasn't my husband and, fact is, I didn't know much about the man.

Truth be told, I didn't never plan to have a husband. Like so many things in my life, I just had to get used to his being in the room when I was washing naked. I didn't like it, but what could I do? I couldn't even accuse him of peering at me 'cause I couldn't even see if he was, but Mrs. Desmets knew.

I couldn't not bathe, although I thought about it 'cause we was taught that "cleanliness was next to Godliness" and I always took that admonition serious. The preacher also preached about modesty, but I was being modest. It made me angry but even anger was a sin so I didn't know where to turn on all these preachings and had no one I could trust to ask.

One night after I had fallen into a restless sleep from thinking about whether my grandmother was still alive and if I could contact her and ask her to come get me, I heard someone coming into my room. I knew from the smell it was Mr. Desmets. He didn't do anything as far as I could tell. I heard him leave a few minutes later and I began to get scared. The next morning I asked him direct in front of Mrs. Desmets, "Mr. Desmets," I said louder than I usually spoke, "What was you doin' in my room last night? Did you want something? If so, you could of asked me, I was awake."

He didn't respond at first until Mrs. Desmets started to say something. Then he interrupted her and said, "I just came into see you was okay. Anything wrong in that? You're my foster and I have responsibility to care for you as well. Just wanted to be sure you was okay."

I knew better and I expected Mrs. Desmets did too.

Just before Christmas, Mrs. Desmets got a letter telling her her brother in Scott City had the ague and was most likely dying. Scott City was fifty miles as the crow flies, but crows don't carry people so the trip was a good 100 miles by truck. I begged Mrs. Desmets to let me go with her, promising to help and offering up all the things I might do to make her time with her brother easier, but it was decided by everyone but me that I would stay put. Mr. Desmets would drive her over to Scott City, spend one night and then return home. I'd see to the animals and the chores. Then in a week, Mr. Desmets would go back and fetch Mrs. Desmets regardless of how her brother was feeling. There was no phone in the Desmets household and I didn't know if her brother had a phone.

This really scared me, being in the house alone with Mr. Desmets. I couldn't ascertain his intentions around me, but didn't like what I was fearing. After the truck left the yard and I counted to fifty to make sure they was beyond seeing the farmhouse. I rushed upstairs and packed my few things into my valise and left. I had a Hoover cane that I hadn't much used, but had been trained on at the school, but I couldn't find it so I stole a yard stick from the kitchen and set out. It took me awhile to find the road, 'cause the yard was flat dirt and felt just like road. When I finally felt where the road led off the yard, I set out.

I walked on the shoulder 'cause I could feel the difference between the dirt road and the shoulder with its grass and weeds sprouting. I walked all morning until I came to an intersection, but I didn't know which way to turn so I asked God and I think he said to go to my left so I did and followed that road for a long time. I could feel the sun going down and the chill coming on. At least there wasn't no snow yet.

Finally, in the far distance I heard a car comin' down the road from behind me. I stopped and moved sidewise to be more on the shoulder off the road and not be in the way. The car was comin' fast and I could hear it slowin' down. The driver pulled up, near me, rolled down his window and asked if I needed a lift. I was very scared then. I allowed as I didn't need a ride, but needed to know how far it was to town?

"What town?" came the answer.

"The nearest town," I answered back.

"You have no idea where you're going to, do you little girl."

"I ain't a little girl and I'm going to Kansas City," I declared as no other place came to mind.

"That's a mighty long way. You walkin' the whole way?" asked the driver.

"If I have to, yes," I shot back.

"Ain't you the Desmets foster kid?" the driver asked.

"Yes, I was," I answered, "but I'm on my own now and going to stay with my grandmother."

"And she lives in Kansas City, right?"

"Yes, I believe she does," I answered again.

"But you're not sure."

Hard as I fought it, I began to cry. Funny how much we don't control in our lives. I wanted not to cry more than anything, but the sobs just kept heavin' out of me.

"Get in and I'll give you a ride back home. I know Hetty and Elroy, and they'd miss you something terrible if you left. Do they know you're gone?"

"Mrs. Desmets brother is ailin' in Scott City and they drove up there. Mr. Desmets'll be back home tomorrow night."

"We live just down the road. You wanna spend the night with Millie and me?"

I didn't get no fear from the man's voice, but decided being alone at the Desmets would be safer 'cause I knew it and I accepted the man's offer to drive me home. He said it was seven miles back and I was too tired and thirsty to think of anything else.

Turned out the fellow was nice enough. He told about his own kids. He had a girl seven and a boy ten, named Martha and Jake. I said I'd like to meet them sometime and play with them and that I could even teach them some things. He asked how old I was and I told him I was fifteen, but that I'd be sixteen in June. When we got to the house, he said he'd be in touch about me meeting his kids, but I knew from his tone that he wouldn't 'cause he'd made a remark on the way back about the Desmets being loners and not socializing much, even when they was tradin' or at church. Him sayin' that made me feel even more alone. I stood outside and listened to his car drive off down the road until I didn't hear it no more.

I couldn't face going back into that house even though there was no one there. I remembered I had to do the animal chores so I did them after I got a glass of water and went inside to have some hard tack and butter for dinner. I also ate two apples as they was fresh and crisp from new picking. Then I got out the basin and had a cold bath in the kitchen. It was the only time I felt like I was in privacy. The water warmed up after I sat in it for awhile and I just enjoyed sittin' there and the safety of being alone even though I knew it wouldn't last.

That night I slept fitfully again and kept dreaming that Mr. Desmets was in the room. The next morning I had some apples and rhubarb conserve on hard tack and tidied up as best I could. I did the animal chores early and brought in a half-dozen eggs from the henhouse. I don't know why but those hens seemed like the only friends I had there. When I'd come into their yard, they'd all flock around me and start gabblin' about this and that, like they was commentin' on how tall I was or how pretty I was or what all until they all got busy peckin' at the cracked corn I'd throwed 'em.

By mid-afternoon I was apprehensin' about Mr. Desmets coming home. He arrived about 6:30 and seemed very tired. With no greeting, he asked me what was for supper and I told him I'd make him whatever he wanted if I knew how. He huffed and told me to bring him some bread, butter, and a slice of ham from the Frigidaire. I got the ham and sliced off a thick piece, put in on a plate with a dollop of butter and a piece of bread. I got him a fork and knife and put the plate on the table where I thought he was sitting.

"Over here," I heard and moved the plate to where he was sitting.

"A glass of milk, too," I then heard and I got him a glass of milk from the jar of milk we kept in the Fridge.

"D'jou do all 'em chores?" he asked.

I told him I did.

"Ain't chou eatin'?" he said.

"I already et," I answered. "I'm gonna turn in early."

"Why you so tired? Don't look like you done much while I was gone."

"Did the best I could and I'm tired. Good night Mr. Desmets,"

"How come you don't call me daddy ever or at least Elroy?" he said in what I thought was threatening.

"Just being polite like they taught us in school and in church," I answered. "Can I go to bed now?"

"Seems early to me, but go ahead if you've a mind to. I got to check the animals."

I hie'd myself up to my room and snuggled into bed as fast as I could. I began talking to Anna like she was right there with me. About an hour later, I heared Mr. Desmets yell up the stairs, "Who you talkin' to up there. You got someone with ya?"

I waited a minute and told him I musta been talkin' in my sleep. I didn't hear no more from him that night.

While Mrs. Desmets was away, I tried extra hard to please Mr. Desmets and to make him like me by waitin' on him as best I could and by bein' pleasant and conversing with him. With Mrs. Desmets away, he did seem to talk more to me and in a nicer tone than before. I began to feel that things would work out between us and he even offered me half of a Hershey bar one night after supper. I began to sleep better and more secure.

The fourth night, it happened. I awoke sensing him in my room again and before I knew it, he was in my bed and pulling at my nightshirt. I can't tell the rest 'cause it's too bad and I don't have the words for telling it. It happened every night until the day before he left to get Mrs. Desmets. He told me not to tell her or he'd see I was sent to the juvenile delinquent home and that I'd never get out.

After he left, I couldn't get out of bed the next day and I could feel my bed was full of blood. I could smell it and feel its wet stickiness. I could also smell him and the stink of his body and sweating on me.

When I finally got up, it hurt just to walk. I went out to the privy, but on the way there I thought I'd faint. I got disoriented and missed it, standing in the rhubarb patch, which I knew was twenty feet to the right and I had to walk back until I found it. I stayed in there for a half hour and throwed up as well.

Mr. Desmets was gone. I could hear the tractor way off in the field. It was dog days and the weather was warmer than usual so I just took off my night shirt and got under the outside tap. I washed and washed, but I couldn't wash off the smell. I think the smell of him took up in me, even though I washed hard with lye soap.

The next two nights, I didn't fight like I did the first night and he seemed to lose interest in molestin' me. The last night he didn't come in at all but I don't think I slept at all that night.

When he left and I couldn't hear the truck motor any more, I went in and tore my sheets off the bed and brought them down. I shaved a bunch of lye soap into the bath basin with a paring knife and filled the tub with cold water from the tap.

I scrubbed at the sheets until my hands was raw and then hung 'em out to dry in the sun. Then I took another bath in fresh water. I didn't like to use the stove when there was no one around 'cause I couldn't always tell how the fire was doin' in the firebox or when the water was boilin' without sticking my finger in it.

Mr. Desmets didn't tell me when he left. Fact is, he never spoke another word to me after the first night. Perhaps, he was too ashamed of himself. I'll never know and I don't care. I hated him for what he done to me. I didn't understand it and never knew a man could have so much pent-up hatred for another person and violence in him.

I was alone for the next three days and apart from the fear of not knowing if I'd ever see the Desmets again, I was happy to be alone. If I'd had food and a ride to church singing, I'd a been content to spend the rest of my life alone unless I knew where I could find Anna.

I was having sliced apples and raw carrots I dug from the garden and some stale bread and butter for supper when I heard the distant sound of the truck motor. I prayed to God Mrs. Desmets was in that truck as I am not sure I would have cared to live through another time alone with Mr. Desmets. I heard two sets of footsteps come up onto the front porch and thanked God. They came in and no one even said hello, not even Mrs. Desmets. I learned later that her brother, Ernest, had died and they had stayed on for the funeral since it was such a long way. I was just as happy. I paid my regrets to Mrs. Desmets who mumbled something about her brother being in the hands of our Lord now and about a better place, but said nothing else.

The next few days were strange. Mrs. Desmets went silent like her husband. I didn't tell what happened 'cause I was scared and didn't know what Mr. Desmets might do if I told what he'd done to me. There was hardly no talking except what was necessary to make the things of a day happen, talk of kitchen, laundry, animal and cleaning chores. At first, I was fearsome and then suddenly, I wasn't anymore. I figured that Mr. Desmets was shamed somehow by his actions against me and that Mrs. Desmets was sad about losing her brother. I was happier in the silence, though I couldn't read anyone's moods like I can when they're conversin'.

Winter came on hard and fast after Thanksgiving. It snowed about six inches. The privy was freezing cold and I made a point of going there only twice a day if I could manage. We didn't celebrate Thanksgiving at all. I remember Mrs. Desmets putting three cold plates on the table each with a bologna sandwich and some butter that tasted rancid to me.

I lay in bed that night recalling the Thanksgiving Anna and me had at the

School for the Blind. It was grand with turkey and gravy and stuffing and mashed potatoes and yams and sweet peas. Before dessert, everyone had to say one thing they was grateful for and I said my friendship with Anna. There was pies for dessert and we sang hymns of praise and thanksgiving after dinner and stayed up late telling stories of what we remembered from our earlier days. I guess there was no money for Thanksgiving or maybe the Desmets didn't know it was Thanksgiving. I wasn't going to tell them 'cause I didn't have much to be thankful for at that time in my life.

The winter came on even harder before Christmas and I realized I was trapped. At least I felt a little safer with Mrs. Desmets in the house even though I still had to do my bathing in front of Mr. Desmets, who only went outside then to feed the animals or to bring in stove wood.

I relied on Mrs. Desmets to warn me when my period was starting by telling me there was spotting in my under things. I still didn't have a brassiere even though my breasts was getting bigger and I should have had one. I got so I counted between my monthlies and would put the rag on anyway even without her telling.

Then I began to feel nauseous like I did when Mr. Desmets done that to me and my breasts began to hurt. I was too proud to say anything to Mrs. Desmets who seemed even quieter than before. I began to wonder if she was still mournin' her brother 'cause the only mention of him I'd heard before he died was that he was out of work and living in a boarding house. Otherwise, she never spoke of him.

Soon, I began to fear the unnatural quiet and worried that Mr. Desmets might find a time when Mrs. Desmets was not looking to come into my room again. My one encouragement was knowing that she couldn't drive and couldn't do her trading in town without Mr. Desmets driving her so I wouldn't be left alone with him and I didn't think he would try again what he done to me with her in the house since there was so much racket from it and I would have screamed for help.

After my birthday, I realized I was with child but didn't say anything. At first, I cried myself to sleep every night, but it was silent crying so as not to attract their attention. I figured that if Mrs. Desmets knew it'd be the same as my telling her, and Mr. Desmets would carry out his threat to send me to the juvenile home and that I'd spend the rest of my life there. I never felt so scared and not knowing what to do. Usually, I'd been pretty independent and resourceful figurin' on things, but this felt like I'd fallen into some kind of trap that I couldn't get out of. I didn't have no one to write to, didn't know any addresses. I was taught how to use a phone at the School, but there was no phone and no one to call. Besides you had to know a number or a name and place.

I talked silent to Anna even though she wasn't there.

I knew I'd be showin' soon and, try as I could, I knew it would be hard to hide it from Mrs. Desmets. That's what I feared most. Lucky, all I had was my worn old jumper 'cause it hung loose on me, but I'd growed a lot and my bosom was filling out the top and it got harder to even fit into it. It was the same jumper I was wearing when I came there.

Finally, one night at dinner — I think we was almost into March — Mrs. Desmets says "Well, I see you got 'cherself with child. That's a pretty mess you done."

I felt an anger rise up in me that I never felt before. I lost all my fear. Maybe the Lord was in me with his righteousness.

"How do you suppose that happened?" I flashed at her. "You suppose I done it to myself?"

I didn't care what happened to me anymore. I figured I'd be better off in the detention than in this graveyard house.

There was a long silence and Mrs. Desmets finally broke the silence.

"Elroy told me how you prancied around naked while I was gone and acted like a Jerusalem harlot to try and draw him to you. I can't blame my man for what you brought on him."

I just started crying. I never felt so defeated in my life. I see'd how it would all play out. My cryin', a' course, sounded like confessing and, either way, I was beat.

I had enough anger to tell the truth and hoped and prayed I would be taken from that house and that loveless couple.

"While you was gone, your husband came into my room three times and had on me in a terrible way. I done nothing to bring it on him. It was his doing and he should be ashamed taking that kind of advantage of a blind child."

There was a long silence during which I imagined they was talkin' in faces the way sighted people do when they don't want a blind person to know what they's sayin'.

Finally, I heard Mrs. Desmets say, "You vamped my husband while I was gone and betrayed all the good we brung you. You should be ashamed and the devil will claim your soul and your baby's."

I got up from the table, spilling my milk on the floor, and went up to my room.

I was too angry to cry. I just lay there like a tipped over gravestone in a graveyard. I couldn't cry. Mercifully, I fell asleep and slept without dreams until the next day. When I went downstairs there was no one there.

A few days later, a car or truck pulled up. I'd lost all my fear at this point. There was a knock on the door. Mrs. Desmets answered and a woman came in and introduced herself. She said she was from the state and she was here to pick up a girl named Nadine Hoover. I was so happy. I came forward and said. "I'm Nadine."

There was no formalities. I collected my things, grabbed an apple off the table, walked outside, and got in the car by the front porch. I sat in the front seat and waited.

I didn't want to hear Mrs. Desmets filling that woman's head with her lies. I didn't have any fear about where I went after being in that Godforsaken house.

After a short time, the woman came out and got in the driver's seat. She introduced herself as Miss Shannon and explained she was from the Foster Care Agency and that she was going to take me to a doctor for a checkup and to confirm that I was pregnant. Course, we both knew I was pregnant.

After a few miles a' quiet driving, Miss Shannon asked me what happened in the house and I told her in all the detail I could muster. I told her that I knew Mrs. Desmets blamed it all on me.

"They always do," she answered to my astonishment. "You see, they ain't got anything at all 'cept their sad husbands, bad as they might be. It's all they got in the world and they'se so afraid a' losin' what little they got, they tell lies and try to believe different from what's true."

At first, I didn't understand.

"You mean you believe me over her?" I asked.

"Yes," she answered quietly. "I do. I seen it before. Your papers say you're just fifteen. Is that right?"

"Yes," I answered. "I had my birthday in January, course they didn't know it."

"We're going to see that you're okay."

I just started crying again beyond control. I hated that feeling of not being able to hold back my tears. They just came in sobs and deep breaths. I hadn't felt cared for at all since I left the school.

Miss Shannon took me to another foster, but there was only a woman there and there was other girls stayin' there. It sounded like a big house when I went in and there was lots of steps up to the porch. I could hear other girls. She introduced a Mrs. Metcalf, sayin' she was the housemother and there was no men here and she would take care of me for a few days until I had seen the doctor and arrangements could be made to take me to the Briller Maternity Lying-in Home in Topeka.

First thing I did after settlin' into a room with a young girl named Daisy was to take a long soak in the big bathtub at the end of the hall. I asked about washin' up and was told I could take a bath anytime I wanted. I had never had that luxury and ended up taking a bath each day of the three days I was there. The hot water came right out of the tap after lettin' it run for a little. I'd turn on the hot water only and it'd run cold for a while and then get real hot and by the time it got to the right temperature, I'd shut it off with my feet. There wasn't no time limit either. I could a stayed in that tub until someone else wanted to use it.

I felt my body all over which I hadn't done very much 'cause I was so occupied with other worries. I'd changed a lot, not only in the womanly places, but also in my arms and legs. My hair was longer and I wondered if I was beautiful. Oh, and there was sweet smellin' soap and a fingernail brush and a big, old, scratchy towel for dryin' off. I had never had such luxuries, not even at the school. I could a stayed here for the rest of my life.

Daisy didn't say much and so I didn't have much conversing with her. She seemed like she was either shy or had been hurt somehow. I could tell she was younger and I wasn't about to try and get her talk if she didn't have a mind to.

There was kind folks what came and went during the day, all women, and three meals a day, and girls to talk to. I knew that some of them were pregnant like me, but others were too small to be. Course, I thought I was too, but began to be excited about the idea of being a mother and having a baby of my own, even though I had no idea how I'd care for it.

I'd gotten up a real fear of men in me from Mr. Desmets, but the doctor was nice enough. Oh, I supposed there was nice men in the world like the preacher in Bazine or the people in some books, but I couldn't see their faces and or know their intentions about me until it was too late. I could only judge from the sound of their voice or, if they was close enough, their smell and some men was deceivin' in their voice and would sound and smell all nice, but would have bad intentions toward me, I learned soon enough. I'd met weak women, but never met a bad woman what had evil intentions against me.

The doctor wanted to look at my parts that I'd been taught no man should ever look at, even if he was your husband. I'd been so violated I didn't care so much. I just did what he told me. He was gentle and spoke kindly to me. He told me I was going to have a baby and that I was probably ten or twelve weeks pregnant. He said I looked healthy and was glad I kept myself clean. He asked me some personal questions which I won't tell here and I answered 'em direct, as I seemed to be losin' my fear more.

The following week Mrs. Shannon came again. I was glad to see her, as she was the only person I met that ever believed me over a grow'd up person. She was takin' me to the train station where she explained I would travel unescorted to Topeka where someone would meet me and take me to the Brill as she called it. After my time at the Desmets, I was just grateful to be going to a place where there'd be other people and I'd feel safe, and like I was cared for. She told me it was a kindsome place and that I'd be safe and well looked after until my baby came.

As much as I hated to leave Mrs. Metcalf's house, I was lookin' forward to my next sojourn at the Brill Home for unwed mothers. If'n it was half as nice as my time at the School for the Blind, it'd be a hundred times better than my time at the Desmets.

The train ride was especially fun. I sat next to a woman who was travelin' to see her mother in Topeka and 'cause I was blind, took on describin' the countryside we was travelin' through. Her words was like the words of someone who writes books because as she described the colors and fields and the sky, I began to have pictures on what farmin' country in Kansas looked like.

When we'd stop in a town to pick up passengers, she'd describe the people getting on and off the train with their bundles, the station, a diner, and the shops along the main street if she could see them. I especially liked it when she told of a mother in all her finery and her little girl dressed up in a pinafore with curly hair which she described, holding her little dolly and waitin' for the train to stop so she could get off. I never met anyone who could do describin' in words so well that pictures'd come up in my mind like they did with her. I can't remember her name, but it was something like Miss Ellie. I remember her voice and words like they was yesterday.

Anyway, we got to Topeka and she helped me off the train with my valise, which was a little heavier now, as Mrs. Metcalf and Miss Shannon had got me some clothes that fit me. They also got me a brassiere and some underthings that was more designed for a woman than a little girl. It was the first time where I didn't have to put on the same things every day. Oh, how I wish I could a' seen myself in my new clothes in a mirror. I never really know'd what I looked like and I wondered how I looked compared to the little girl that Miss Ellie described on the train.

Unlike in Bazine, a woman came right up to me on the platform and asked if I was Nadine and I said proudly. "I am Nadine."

She took my hand and led me off the platform to a car like she knew about blind people. She didn't say much, but I felt comfortable with her, like she know'd what she was doin' and with whom.

Folks seemed to call the Home for unwed mothers the "Brill," which was short for Briller Maternity Lying-in Home, which is hard to say.

I shared a room with another girl named Lula Dell Bonner. She was seventeen and seemed very nice, but shy at first. She was from Emporia, Kansas. She said she'd got pregnant by her boyfriend, who told her that she couldn't get pregnant if they only had sex on certain days. This was all more than I had ever heard about girls and boys and, at first, it made me uncomfortable, but then I got interested even though I never had a boyfriend and never wanted to have one. When she told him she was going to have a baby and they could get married, he up and disappeared.

He was nineteen and joined the service she later learned from his sister, di'n't say goodbye or nothin', just gone. Her minister counseled her and her parents about her sin and she got sent to the Brill. I came to learn that a lot a girls got told lies about bein' with boys and came here 'cause they hadn't been told truthful about boys, either by the boys themselves or by their mothers. Course, from my own experience it's the girl what gets blamed for the whole business. Who do folks think stuck it in 'em? I shouldn't talk like that, but it makes me hellish angry. Bein' an ordained minister and all, I try to watch my words and try and speak kind to all folks even when I get up a righteous anger on something.

They was nice at the home and there was no men anywhere for me to worry about. Only men allowed on the property was a groundskeeper, the doctor, and sometimes outside repair men and they always had to be accompanied by the matron or, in the doctor's case, a nurse.

I came to find out there was two kinds a' girls at the Brill. Them, like me, that was scared and distrustful of men, 'cause a' their experience with 'em, and there was girls that was crazy on 'em, always talkin' about 'em. Always wishin' they was with a man, like they had an itch down there that constantly needed scratchin'. They'd dance to the radio together in the common room and practice flirtin' like one was a man and the other a woman. I'd never heard anything like it. The matron did everything she could to discourage it, but some of them girls was just boy-crazy and wasn't even thinkin' on what had happened to 'em and who done it to 'em.

Lula was quiet. We never got like me and Anna, but we did become friends. She was just shy and didn't say as much about herself as Anna and me did. Course, I was younger, too.

Days at the Brill were always the same. They made a half-heart attempt to teach girls that wanted to learn, but it was mostly about comportment and hygiene. There was no book-learning or classes like at the other school and a' course, they wasn't used to a blind girl like me. There was two girls there that was deaf-mute, but I didn't hear tell of any blind girls. There was 126 girls in the home and it was crowded. The larger rooms had been turned into wards with four or six beds and there wasn't hardly room to turn around. Some girls, especially them that was close to deliverin', spent most of their days in bed. There was a doctor there who seemed kindly enough and six nurses. He never came into the dorm rooms unless it was an emergency. Always the girls went to his examining room for their doctor visits.

When birthin' time came, the girls was hustled to a small surgery next to his office and a midwife and nurses would deliver the baby unless there was complications and the doctor would come in and help. Course, it was the first time birthin' for all the girls so sometimes there was complications and a girl might have to be taken by car to the hospital in Topeka. Sometimes they said a girl might lose a baby and I hoped that wouldn't happen to me.

In my seventh month there, I began to hear rumors that girls didn't get to keep their babies unless their parents approved and I began to worry 'cause I didn't have any parents to approve my keepin' my baby. I had never had any other plan and would often lie in bed thinkin' on what kind of baby I would have, how I'd love and care for it, like I hadn't been. I secretly hoped the Lord would give me a girl, but assured him that if it was a boy, I'd raise it good and teach him to be a good boy when he growed into a man. If it was a girl, I was going to name her Anna.

About a month before we was expected to deliver, we'd have a meeting with the matron and the way the girls told it, she would make a decision about whether or not you got to keep your new baby. I wouldn't have come there if I had any thoughts that I couldn't keep my baby. I was sure, though, that when matron heard me out, she'd know that I'd be a good mother and let me keep and raise my baby.

In my sixth month, I began to have bad pains and stomach sickness. The nurse said it was 'cause I was young for givin' birth, even though I was almost as tall as Lula. I was still skinny then and not like I am now.

I was just as happy not seeing the doctor, but the pains in my back'd sometimes keep me awake at night and then I could hardly rouse myself to refectory for meals. The food all seemed to make me sick, 'cept on occasion they'd serve pieces of fresh fruit or a fruit compote that I loved. The juicy taste of those fruits was like a balm on my poor stomach and I could sometimes see colors when I was savorin' a peach or an orange.

Other than apples, I hadn't ever had much fruit and even to this day fruits are a special treat for me.

In my eighth month, it got easier to keep down food and I didn't have such sickness when I smelled a plate of food. My breasts began to ache though, 'cause they'd grown bigger than I ever imagined they could and they ached and made my back pains worse. I couldn't get comfortable in bed to sleep and I'd sometimes doze off in a chair during the day 'til I was roused up to go to a meal or an assembly.

My meeting with the matron didn't go good and I began to make secret plans to leave the Brill. She tried to be comfortin', but she had already made up her mind 'bout me givin' up my baby for adoption, perhaps 'cause I had no kinfolk to speak for me. I knew, though, that I had no intention of giving up my baby to anyone.

She carried on and on about how single mothers with no prospects or a job couldn't care for and raise a child, like I'd need a man to help me do that. In my little experience, no man ever added much to rearin' a child, just to breedin' 'em, and, if a girl was lucky, not abusin' 'em. She carried on about all the nice families with nice homes what couldn't have children who'd be so happy to have my baby and raise 'em right like I couldn't. I got so mad that I just let her mouthin' die out in my head like a freight train disappearing into the night. I just sat there bobbin' my head back and forth as blind folks do, but I was a thousand miles away from that woman and her lies.

That night, I made plans to get away from there and to try and find my grandmother, but I couldn't remember the town outside of Kansas City she lived in and I didn't have no money to buy a train ticket. I just knew that a train went from Topeka to Kansas City.

I decided to work out the details later, but, as I got closer to havin' my baby, I knew it'd be harder to travel. The aches and pains already made it hard for me to walk the long corridors, but least I wasn't feelin' sick from the food anymore. My plan was to leave in the night and walk to a neighborhood where I would just go from door to door and tell my story until someone would take me in and help me find my grandmother. I had just a few weeks so I decided to leave the following night.

I knew from the fire drills that the two doors at either end of the home were never locked. I didn't confide my plan to anyone. Lula had had her baby and I didn't even get to say goodbye when she went into labor and was taken down to the surgery. After you had your baby, you was taken to a special ward, I learned, and was kept separate from the girls still waitin' to deliver.

Now, I began to suspect why. As soon as she'd had her baby, another girl named Ella moved in, but I hadn't got to know her and didn't try to, since I knew I'd be leavin'. I was polite and made her feel welcome 'cause she was new at the Brill, but I didn't go out of my way to confide with her. Sides, she told me that her boyfriend told her it was called the "bastard factory" when she left and that made me so angry, I couldn't speak to her no more. I'd heard the term "bastard" and I knew that anyone usin' that word didn't know the Godliness of a newborn baby and never would.

The next day during outdoor period, I made some excuse and returned to my room. I went to the shelf where we kept our clothes to get my valise, but, look as I might, I couldn't lay my hands on it. At first, I thought I'd misplaced it, but then, after touching everything in the room, I realized it was gone. Ella's suitcase was gone as well. Things was addin' up in a bad way. I stuffed my clothes into my pillowcase and pushed it all under my cot. It's hard hiding things when you can't see what other folks see.

That night after lights out, I waited in bed. Ella was cryin' and wanted to talk, but I said I was tired and pretended to be asleep. I was tired and it was hard to stay awake, but I was determined to get out of that home before I couldn't. A couple of hours after lights out, I got up. Ella stirred but didn't seem to wake up. I got my pillowcase and snuck out of the room. It's impossible sneaking when you're blind 'cause you don't know if lights is on or off, if you're sneaking down a hallway and folks is standin' by just watchin' you, or nothing. I prayed to the Lord that I was alone. I knew from hearsay there was no night guards, just the night nurses on duty and they tended to stay in the dispensary and gossip and smoke cigarettes unless someone came askin' for help.

I walked down the stairs at the end of the hall and that was troublesome 'cause the stairs creaked something awful, but there was nothing to be done. I learned at the Desmets to accept what I can't fix. It was the hardest lesson I think I ever learned, but I wasn't done learnin' it.

I pretended that Anna was with me and we was sneakin' out of the School for the Blind together to go to a church meeting where they sang a lot of get-up and go songs, not all about Jesus neither; some of 'em was about dancin' and havin' fun. I often thought to myself, "What's the point of churching that makes you feel guilty and miserable all the time you're tryin' to get to heaven?"

I was worried that what I heard about the doors not being locked might not be true, even though I knew they wasn't supposed to lock people in because of some awful fires that had happened and people got killed 'cause they couldn't escape the flames. The doors weren't locked. I just walked out into the cool evening air. I remembered somewhat the layout of the place and headed for what I thought might be the road where we'd come in. I tripped a couple of times on a curb 'cause I didn't have my Hoover stick. When you're blind, you walk like you're going to trip every time, draggin' your feet, so I didn't fall much. It's only what surprises you that trips you up. But being so heavy and carrying my personals in a pillowcase didn't make it any easier.

I heard a radio in the distance. It was playin' city dance music and I aimed for it. I figured folks listening to that kind of music would understand my worries and maybe would help me find my grandmother. I fell twice going towards that music. Once on a steep curb and again when I ran into a mailbox. At least I knew I was nearin' a house. I'd scuffle my feet in front of me takin' small steps and that way keep from runnin' into things. The music was getting louder and then I came to some steps which I hoped was porch steps. I reached down and felt and the rough planks made four steps. I walked up. There was no handrail and I slowed until I came to a screen door. The hard door was opened, 'cause the music was pretty loud. I knocked on the side of the door.

I don't think they could hear me over the radio music so I asked loudly for some help. Next I heard the radio turn down and then a kindly voice say, "Why honey, whatever's the matter?" I immediately felt relieved that a woman answered the door. I heard the screen door open and felt a warm hand in mine and a voice saying, "Come on in, honey and sit down and you can tell me what kind of help you need. It's late, but I'm sure we can figure on it."

She led me to a divan and sat down next to me. She offered to take my pillowcase, but I said I'd rather keep it with me as it was all I had, and sometimes sighted folks don't understand how blind folks need to keep their things where they know they can find them.

She asked me what the matter was and what help I needed. I didn't tell her that I had come from the Brill, but only that I was looking for my grandmother who would help me with my birthin' and takin' care of my baby. I explained that she was in Kansas City and that I needed to call her and ask where she lived so I could take the train to her and that I knew she'd meet me, but that I had lost her phone number. Course, I wasn't even sure she had a phone.

The kindly lady asked me my name and I told her my name was Nadine Hoover and that I was lost. Oh, how naïve I was. She asked me the name of my grandmother, but all I ever knew her as was "Grannie Hoover." If

I ever did know her last name I couldn't recall it.

She asked me when my baby was due and I told her in a few weeks so I needed to get to my grandmother's soon. To be honest I wasn't quite sure when. Sometimes it felt like any minute. I'm not the kind to make up stories that ain't true, but I was worried she might think I came from the Brill, so I told her my husband was in the service and he was meeting me at my grandmother's to be there for the birthing.

She said she thought that was nice. She said it would be hard to call a big city like Kansas City for information about my Grannie Hoover and asked again if I didn't know where she lived. I explained that she lived just outside the city in a neighborhood, but that I couldn't remember. She asked if she worked somewhere and I said she took in ironing and sewing.

The nice lady asked if I was thirsty and might like some lemonade. I said I would and told her I liked the music too. She fetched me a tall glass of lemonade with some ice in it and a spring of mint. It was the best tastin' thing I think I ever had and the sobs began to well up in me the way they always did when some expressed kindness to me, but I kept them to myself with only a few hiccups.

The nice lady said she would try and call Kansas City information and see what she could find out about where my grandmother lived. The phone was in her bedroom and she left me on the couch to call. Least that's what I thought. Not fifteen minutes later there was a knock on the door and it was two nurses from the Brill come to fetch me back.

I lost all faith in people and the sobs just overtook me. I never felt so betrayed in my life. I later found out that the nice lady was head of the kitchen crew and that runaways sometimes stopped at her house for help, not knowin'. Course it was even harder for a blind person. I thought I'd walked much further, but I was only a little ways from the Brill. I must 'ave doubled back.... No way to tell.

I just cried and cried. The cook lady said she was sorry, but that it was all for the best that I go back and have my baby in a safe place. The nurses took me firmly by either arm and led me to a car outside and drove me back. Ella woke up and asked what happened and the nurses told her I'd tried to escape and all, but they also made their point that no one ever does.

Back in my bed, I couldn't sleep at all. I was cryin' so hard inside but didn't make any sound 'cause I didn't want to get caught up with Ella and her problems that she was wantin' to talk about. I must've fallen asleep 'cause I woke up the next mornin'.

I was put on "runaway watch" which I'd heard about, but I didn't know what it meant. The matron told me there was no way out and that all the neighbors of the Brill was on the lookout for runaway girls. Being blind would make it even harder for me she said. If I tried again, they would have to lock me in my room at night.

I never felt so alone and so hopeless. I resolved then that if I couldn't escape that I would try even harder to get them to let me keep my baby.

That too failed. I kept trying to see the matron. I'd talk to the nurses and they'd just answer, "It's all for the best," which didn't tell me nothin'. It was like everybody smiled and nobody cared about me and my baby.

A few weeks later during afternoon rest, I began to have a lot of pains and by supper time, I was soaked down there. They'd explained to us somewhat what would happen so I knew my water had broke. I asked Ella to get the nurse which she did. They took me into the surgery where babies was delivered. I don't know how long I was laborin' but I first heard my baby cry late in the night. I was exhausted and hurt all over, but that little cry just woke me upright. I lifted my head up and heard another nurse cut the cord and they took the baby in another room.

I panicked and said I wanted to hold it. The nurse smiled and said, we're just washin it up and checkin' fingers, toes and for jaundice and such. I lay back down and waited. After ten minutes, I asked again. The nurse said just a few more minutes and I could see her. That was only how I ever came to know it was a little girl. I named her Anna in my head and wanted to tell the nurse, but she had gone out of the room again. The doctor came in to check me out to see if there was too much bleeding. He gave me a shot that he said would dull the pain 'cause he had to do some sewing down there to help me heal up.

Next thing I knew, I woke up in a hospital bed. I thought I was still in the Brill, but couldn't be sure. I called for a nurse to bring Anna to me so I could start nursin' her. I didn't know how long I'd been asleep. I felt very groggy, but my wantin' to hold Anna cut through all the blurriness.

A nurse I'd never seen before came in and said she's already gone to a new home. She was kindly towards me and whispered that I had given birth to a baby girl and that she had had a full head of beautiful dark brown hair, and that her features were not only normal, but beautiful. Course this didn't help me none even though she was wantin' to be kind. She explained that the Brill didn't allow any contact between mothers and their newborns, as it would only make matters worse. "For who," I answered angrily even though I was still in my grogginess.

Then, a long yowl came outta me like I never heard. It was the kind a' yell that comes from some place you don't know is inside you. After the first yell which wasn't any word, I just kept calling, "Anna, Anna, Anna."

The nurse came back with the doctor who held me down and gave me another shot. Next time I woke, I was in a room alone. It must have been the part of the building where they kept mothers after they did their birthin'. I know'd then they didn't want us tellin' the other girls how it goes and how they take your baby away without you ever seein' it, or holdin' it, or hearin' it, or smellin' it, or nursin' it.

I just wanted to die. I had no one to talk to. No one I knew on the face of God's earth cared for me and the only person I wanted to care for was gone. I stayed in that room for three days and then was told to come to the matron's office.

She said I would be remanded to the foster agency again and would be sent to a new family where I would be taken care of. I sassed back at her that I'd been taken care of once by a family and that's how I ended up here. I told her I didn't want no fake mother and father to use me and that I wanted to be with my grandmother. She told me if I could give them a phone number or an address to contact her, they would see if she would take me. Course, I couldn't. So I vowed this time to run away for good.

As I said, runnin' away when you're blind isn't easy and I had to think hard on how I was going to do it.

Miss Shannon came for me the day I was discharged from the Brill. There was so much bad feeling in me that I resolved to follow the Lord's admonition and not say anything bad, but that anger rose up in me like the Lord's own wrath when she asked if they was good to me. I started by saying all polite, "Nice as they could be, I suppose." Then I continued, "when they'se stealin' and sellin' your baby without tellin' you."

I didn't rue my sayin' it one bit. Miss Shannon was silent for a minute. She asked me and I told her. I could feel again those sobs risin' up in me. I waited for Miss Shannon to carry on about the nice home and the people who were better'n me raisin' Anna and givin' her all the things I couldn't. But was those things supposed to replace the love of her own mother? Did Anna need clothes and dolls and schoolin' more than her natural kin? I ask you. I still ask myself today.

Miss Shannon asked if I needed anything. I told her my breasts hurt something terrible and that the bra she bought for me didn't fit anymore and I thought I needed a new one. Course, I knew they hurt so much 'cause I wasn't feedin' my daughter like I should be doin' by nature.

We stopped at a dry goods store and went inside and a nice lady helped me find a bra that fit. I must been leakin' milk cause she asked if I'd just had a baby. I said, "I had," but didn't say more cause I didn't want to start bawlin' again.

She said, "Oh, you look so young to be a mother." Course I had no idea who was in the store watchin' her, but I was so upset, I just said, "I am, thank you for askin' M'am," knowin' full well she wouldn't know what my meaning was, but that Miss Shannon would.

I still get angry sometimes, but with the Lord's help I'm better at keepin' it in me. At fifteen though, I was still full of piss and vinegar, pardon my saying, and no matter what trials and tribulations was visited on me, I knew after what'd been done to me, I could come out the other side.

I got fostered again and they must a' taken better care, 'cause the Jessups was decent folks, I could tell from the start. They already had one foster named Carla who seemed shy until I got to know her better. She was blind also. It seems Mr. Jessup's mother had been blind and they was comfortable bein' with blind folk and, the foster agency had a hard time placing blind kids. Nobody wanted a blind kid, even if it was only a foster.

Like Anna, my roommate at the School for the Blind, not my daughter Anna, who I still fretted on night and day, Carla had been sighted for much of her life and knew what things looked like. Unlike Miss Ellie, who rescued me from the Desmets, she wasn't good though at words and describin'. She couldn't read, but she could name letters. But at least she had a visual memory of things and this comes in handy. Carla was thirteen and I'd just turned sixteen.

We shared a room on the second floor. From what I could tell the house was nice. Carla said she'd only been with the Jessups for half a year or so and assured me that they was very nice people and wanted to do right by us. She said they was good with blind folks and understood what we needed.

I resolved to settle in and not to cause any trouble. I still didn't feel safe 'cause I'd felt this way when I first moved into the Desmets and look what happened.

Mr. Jessup must've had a good job 'cause the Jessups could afford good food and a nice car and the like. There was nice things in their house. Sheets was cleaned regular and the towels in the bathroom was soft and fresh. At Sunday dinner, there was always a linen table cloth and Carla and I was extra careful not to spill. She'd been in a blind school for a little time, but not as long as I had and I took on myself to share with her what practical things I'd learned about blindness coping. I think my own learnin' went deeper'n hers too, because I was never sighted. We both had things to teach each other. I just wish her describin' words was as good as Miss Ellie's.

We was in a small outskirt of Topeka called Carbondale. It was small enough to be called an outskirt but large enough to have its own school. Course, blind kids couldn't go to regular schools so Carla and me just stayed home. The Jessups was good about wanting us to be independent though and we was allowed to go for walks together in the town. We both had walking sticks as Mrs. Jessups called 'em and we had a regular visit from a blind teacher who came once a week to counsel on us about getting on in life and bein' independent. When we was downtown, we'd stop strangers and ask 'em things like where this or that was and folks was always kindly to us, offering to help.

The Jessups was church folks and we went to Sunday service. It must have been a very big church 'cause there was an echo when the minister spoke and I remember walking down a long aisle to get to where we sat on a Sunday morning. Sitting next to each other in church, we'd sing the hymns we knew together and practice harmonizin'. Carla had a good enough voice but wasn't good at makin' up harmonies that suited the words. Course we couldn't read the hymnals. There wasn't no Braille and Carla couldn't read anyway. But I could memory a hymn pretty much after singing it twice.

On Sundays after church, we had what Mr. Jessup called "Sunday dinner." It was always good food: a beef roast, ham, or a chicken, and potatoes with gravy. It seemed like Thanksgiving every Sunday. We was supposed to have family talkin' time at dinner and gradually I began to talk more. I was shy at first and so full of sadness and anger that I was afraid of saying mean things and having the Jessups think I was a bad person, but I couldn't get rid of those feelings about what had happened and me losing my Anna and all.

Sometimes at night, I'd lie in bed and try and imagine where she was. Who was pretendin' to be her mother? I supposed she'd never know nursin' on a mother's breast and havin' lullabies sung to her. I couldn't imagine what kind a house she lived in, but hoped it wasn't anything like the Desmets ole ramshackle. Oh, I worried so in those days.

I told Carla, I didn't want to stay at the Jessups; that I wanted to go out into the world and make my way. I was surprised when she said she wanted to come along. She musta trusted me some. I was glad too 'cause life's got to be easier for two than for one and 'cause she was sighted once and could relate sounds to pictures like I couldn't.

After three or four weeks, I began to have my doubts. Her bein' just thirteen, I didn't know whether she'd be my daughter or my friend and whether she'd help me solve problems or bring on more.

But I began to worry on how to tell Carla that I thought she was too young to go out on her own, with or without me, that there was people she didn't know in the world who often had bad intentions about girls and women and that she wasn't ready to make do in such a world.

I'd have doubts too and get to thinking on how hard it was going to be to leave the Jessups, 'cause not only had they been good to me, but they knew what blind folks needed to get ahead in the world. Mr. Jessups gave us each an allowance of fifty cents a week. That was a lot of money in those days and I kept mine for the bus fare I knew I would need when I left.

The Jessups had a big old Philco console radio that Mr. Jessups was so proud of. On Saturday nights, if we didn't go out to a band concert on the town green or some community supper, we'd just stay at home and listen to *The Make-Believe Ballroom* with Martin Block.

The show was broadcast out of New York City and played all the big bands and radio crooners. I'd never heard those tunes before and began to memory those songs as well. The Dorseys, Louis Armstrong, Nat King Cole, Glenn Miller all had tunes that I liked. The Jessups would sometimes move the coffee table away from in front of the couch and let

Carla and me practice our ballroom dancing together. Sometimes we'd get so excited that we'd bump into a chair or the couch, fall down and we'd all start laughing. The Jessups was good that way about laughing with us, 'stead of at us.

One of my favorite singers was a Negro lady named Una Mae Carlisle. I can still hear in my mind her singin' comin' out of that big Philco: "Tired Hands," "I Bought Myself a Book," "Now I Lay me Down to Dream," and "Tonight Be Tender To Me."

Her deep husky voice was so tender. It would put me in a mind to recall all the losses in my life and make me sad, but in a good way. I learned that feelin' things through was the only way for me to get by.

We never did leave the Jessups. I don't know; they was kind and maybe it was just too comfortable there. I felt safe for the first time since I'd left the School for the Blind and I knew I would betray their kindness if I took up and left without saying anything.

I don't like to hurt people, especially when they're as good to me as the Jessups was. The following spring they sent me to an adult school in Kansas City where they taught the adult blind how to weave baskets and write script. We also had a Bible course.

After summer school was over though, I had no place to go as my time with the Jessups was over. I'd said all my good-byes to them when I left for the school so I was released into the custody of a distant brother-in-law named Henry and a woman named June, but they weren't even really .... I mean they weren't married themselves. It was a common-law marriage. There was nothing wrong with that. But I didn't know they weren't married; I mean I didn't know that there was such a thing as a common-law marriage; I just thought this couple was sharing a place. They had different rooms and it looked very above-board and everything.

Well, next thing I know, this Henry is all interested in me and such and his attentions felt good even after all my bad encounters with men. He made me feel safe and all, like he really cared for me. So well, I finally decided to listen in after I started becoming the mistress of this man, this Henry. I wanted to be sure, even though they was living together, that he wasn't two-timin' her. I listened down and I heard that they was a couple in bed, not just in the apartment. So then I found out I was going to have his baby. So when this woman found out, why she was very angry, and of course I wouldn't tell who the baby belonged to. Shame on me again, I don't know what I was thinkin'. Why, I was as surprised as she was.

Well, I wasn't gonna have no relative's baby, no matter how distant ....
Well, I was — I was gonna have a baby, but I went out and had an abortion before I even began to show I was carryin'. And as often as I thought about my Anna, I wasn't gonna have this two-timin' man's baby. I just had to leave that place. I never even gave two thoughts to ending that pregnancy — the right and wrong and all — seems like I was just fixated on surviving and I didn't want no stranger's baby in me. You'd think I'd have figured out that all that sex led to having babies and such. I was something else in those days — all mixed up I guess.

So then again, I didn't have any place to go. So there was a lady, a blind lady, oh, she was considerable older than me and she offered to take me home with her because she was a Christian lady and she wanted to do a charitable work, and I had no place else to go; so she took me home with her and then she took me to a Bible conference, and this was in Miltonvale, Kansas, and that's where I first learned to be a real Christian, when we went to this Bible conference. So then they got me into Bible school, and that was in Wesleyan College in Miltonvale, Kansas. And I went to that school for two years and took Bible courses and then, after that — 'course I still had no place to go after that because this woman, this Bertha, the blind lady that took me home, her sister just cracked down on her 'cause she wasn't a Christian and she says, "Look now, we can't keep her around here," and she just told Bertha, "You know you had no right to bring her here without consulting me." So I couldn't go back there anymore. So then I was put in the county poor farm. I was twenty-three — yeah, I was twenty-three.

While there, I tried to be helpful, you know; I'd go down to the kitchen, wash the dishes and empty the bedpans for some of the patients that were bedfast, and I'd carry the empty trays, you know, after they got through with them. But I didn't have to do that, you know, I just wanted something to do. And it kinda helped me feel like I was earning my way.

So I was in that poor farm for about, oh, six months, and then — that was after my first year in Miltonvale — I went back to school again, and then after I came back from Miltonvale the second year — let's see, where did I stay after that? Oh, I would stay at Bertha's house part of the time; and then there was other people that took me and 'course finally I got on welfare and my case worker put me in a place, kind of a foster home. It was just a place with a lady; it was called the "Shady Rest Home for the Aged." It was an old folks' home really. So I landed in there 'cause I didn't have anywhere else to go and this woman was supposed to teach me how to work in the kitchen and keep my own apartment, but she didn't; she says, "Aw, you don't have to do that...."

Well, she taught me but she wasn't a very good teacher. She was a very good woman. I loved her very much, but she wasn't a very good teacher. She liked me a lot, and I'd go around to different rooms, from room to room and read the Bible to all the people. And she said one day, she said, "Listen, why don't you gather the people at least once a week and have a little meeting," and I says, "Oh – could I?!" She said, "Of course." So every week then — it was on a Wednesday — we'd all gather in the big front room and then we'd have a little meeting and I'd preach a little sermon.

That was where I started learning to preach, and of course I had the two years of Bible school; but what made me start to do that ... I was praying one day; I was on my knees praying; I was praying for this one and that one, you know, 'cause oh — some of 'em were so sick, and I'd pray, you know, I'd say, "Lord, help Newton, Lord, help Jack," and I'd name 'em all off — and it just seemed like the impression came to me, "But what are you doing about it? What are you doing for them?" and I said, "Lord, but what is there; what can I do for them?" And I got the impression, "Go into the rooms and spread the Word and read the Bible." And I said, "All right, I'll do that." And so then she said, "Instead of having to do that, why, you can just come and have a meeting every week." But still why then they said, "We want the meeting every week, but we want her to come to our rooms, too". So even though I had a meeting once a week, why, every morning I'd go around to each room and read the Bible.

So then the Lord definitely laid on me a real call to preach. And I said — 'course I really argued about it — I said, "Lord, now you know that I can't talk worth a poop." I said, "I'm no good at makin' speeches and deliverin' sermons," I said, "Now, if you want me to preach, you're sure gonna have to help me, 'cause I can't do it." And I thought, "I don't believe it's really the Lord calling me. I think it's just my own imagination." And you know, it just seemed like the people really enjoyed the meetings, they wanted them, and so all the rest of the time I was there I did that.

When I was twenty-six, I got married. I met this guy in summer school. His name was Charles Jerome Martin, but they called him Buzz. And so, of course, I just knew him as Buzz Martin, and so we got married. But when I was twenty-three I had had a hysterectomy, 'cause I had no idea that I was ever gonna get married, and I was havin' such problems with sex.

I was twenty-two when I had the abortion, and then I went on from the abortion into summer school for the first time, and then I went from summer school to this Miltonvale Bible School and then I was having an awful time with sex. My great-uncle had molested me and bothered around. He was a real old man, he was fifty-eight at the time; and so like I say, it was a real problem for me and I thought, "Well God, I might as well have a hysterectomy," and it was, you know, really the worst mistake I ever made in my life. I wish now I hadn't done it.

It was suggested to me by the supervisor of the Miltonvale School of the Wesleyan College Bible School. She said, "Look", — 'course she was a virgin herself; she'd never been... and I think she was kind of jealous of me because I had boyfriends, blind boyfriends. I had two that year and one of them lived in Kansas City and he kept calling me from Kansas City, and the other one lived in Wichita, Kansas, and he kept calling me from Wichita, and it just burnt her up. I'm telling you, when I'd get those long-distance calls, she would just smolder! She said, "Well, one of your boyfriends are calling you again", and 'course she didn't like it — so she suggested that I have a hysterectomy, and I didn't want to.

At first, I thought, "Oh dear no, I don't want to do that," and yet, oh, they kind of talked me into it. When I went out to the poor farm, why the doctor, he said, "Is she sure that's what she wants?" He said that to Miss Fowler; he said that to the superintendent of the poor farm, you know, and Miss Fowler said, "It seems to be what she wants." And you know, I had no one to really sit down and talk to me and say, "Look, Baybie, if you do this, certain things will happen, this will happen, that will happen, and you'll get fat, you won't have any more sex feeling", and I just didn't have anyone to tell me anything, but anyway, so much for that.

Before that, I never weighed more than 120 at the very most. 'Course when I was pregnant and had my baby, I got up to 148, but I quickly got back down 'cause I took exercises and I got back down to my good old 120. I never weighed more than that. It was a good weight for me at 5'2". So anyway, I had this stupid hysterectomy. I guess everybody's entitled to one major mistake, but I'm telling you, I'm not due any more the rest of my life. I mean I made that one and that's enough for about ten or twelve.

So I met this Buzz Martin in the School for the Blind in Kansas City in the summer school, and 'course he lied to me about his age. He told me he was thirty-seven, which, since I was twenty-six, wasn't unreasonable; it was just eleven years. Really, though, he was fifty-two. I found out later because we went back to Lecompton, Kansas, and 'course he'd lived round there all his life.

So, I was gonna have a birthday party for him, and I told Gert, our next-door neighbor, Gert Everetts, I said, "Well, Gert," I said, "I'm gonna have a birthday party for Buzz." And I said, 'I'm gonna get thirty-eight candles." And she said, "Why thirty-eight?" I said, "Well, he's thirty-eight!" She said, "Thirty-eight!" She said, "Baybie, you must have misunderstood him." I said, "Well, what do you mean?" She said, "He's gonna be fifty-three." So ... oh wow!

So I jumped him with it that night. I said, "Listen, Buzz, how come you lied to me about your age?" He said, "Well, I was afraid you wouldn't marry me if I didn't." I said, "Listen, Buzz, there's no girl in the world that's worth lying to get." And I said, "It's not a very good foundation to start a marriage on." And he said, "Are you mad at me?" I said, "What would be the use to be mad at you?" I said, "It's done now," but I said, "You know, it certainly don't make me want to trust you much." I said, "I never can tell if you're gonna be lying to me," and then I caught him in another lie — several lies — and so, it wasn't much of a marriage. And besides, I was so dead sexually.... Oh, that was another funny thing.

Just before I was gonna get married I went to this doctor that had performed the operation. I said, "Look, Dr. Kelly, what just exactly did you do?" He says, "Well, I took everything." I said, "Well, I'm gonna be married." And he just started laughing. He really went into hysterics. I said, "Well. I don't see what you see so funny," I said, "but I'm glad that I'm providing you with a good laugh." He said, "It isn't funny, not really." I said, "Why did you do this without consulting me, without telling me what you were going to do or anything?" He said, "Well. I thought that's what you wanted."

He was an old man and he just laughed and laughed for about two minutes. I guess he was laughing at the irony of life. Yeah, because I'm telling you, life is really something. It'll twist you around. Since I had that hysterectomy, I never had any trouble getting a man. I had so many opportunities to go to bed with a man after I had my hysterectomy, when I didn't give a hoop about it! And then when I was so hot, and, you know, young and strong and full of life, before I had my hysterectomy, a man wouldn't look at me with a ten-foot pole, you know. I was shy I guess, but that's the way life is, you see.

So I said, "Now look, Doctor. I don't have a spark of sex in me." And I said, "You're gonna have to give me some." So he gave me some of this ovarian stuff, ovary capsules. He says, "Listen, I'm gonna tell you something. This is going to make you awful sick." I said, "Oh, great." And it didn't really help much, no. And he said, "It might not help you too much, but we'll try it. I said, "Boy, you really hold out a lot of hope, don't you?" I said, "I never should have had that done."

Right after my hysterectomy, I began putting weight on. I really don't know... I just... I took exercises too. I mean, I used to walk, but I still put on weight. I was seven years getting adjusted to that because, my God, I was so different. I was like two different people. I changed from a very affectionate, spontaneous person to a very calculating... I began to be very computerish... you know. I'd think before I'd do anything, and I'd weigh everything. You know that's not like a young person. And I got where I would just, well... I was all mixed up emotionally. I didn't know from nothing. I didn't know what was happening to me. 'Cause before, when I had felt, you know, and everything was... I had felt everything so keenly, you know, and now everything had to work through the reasoning, through the mind.

But anyway, it was an awful marriage; I mean, I wasn't satisfactory to him, he wasn't satisfactory to me. But we got along as far as.... We were friends and all that.

Virginia, she would come off and on, 'course her father and mother were divorced and she was staying part of the time with one; that is, her mother had kinda, oh, partially forsaken her and kind of put her off with her dad; so she'd — every time she had any money at all — why she'd come to Udall, Kansas, and visit me. Anytime she had money at all, 'nough to pay the rent, why she'd come, stay a week or two with me. And 'course we kept this up.

She was with me lots of times. Buzz would walk with us kids. See, he had his sight before, he was what we call adventitiously blind; in other words, he wasn't congenitally blind, and of course he knew every crevice and cranny around there. He knew how to get around. He'd get around like a wizard and take us to different places, you know, like there was a shut-in, an old lady and she couldn't get out, and I'd go and preach to her. We'd go and have meetings at every place that would have us. Why Buzz would walk us up there and then we'd have our meetings. Then he'd come get us. He was awful good about that; he was a good person.

We didn't live together too long. I got married when I was twenty-six and I started going back to Udall, Kansas and going around. I didn't stay in Lecompton very long. I think we lived together steady for about two years. And, 'cause I couldn't see there was anything in it for him, I just didn't see any use in being a burden to him when I couldn't be a wife to him—I did cook for him and all that; he liked my cooking, but... nah... that wasn't for me ....

Also, I forgot to tell that when Virginia and me walked alone in town or in the neighborhood, we'd practice hymn singing together and work out new harmonies and sometimes people would stop and say a kindly word and put some coins in our hands. People seemed to like our singing together and later that worked its way into our plan for leaving.

I was born on September 24th in Wichita in a large two-story house at 121 South Velutia Street, and my mother and father were divorced when I was nine months old.

When I was born, my mother did not have enough fluid in her body and, not only did she not have enough fluid, but she squeezed herself up in a corset very, very tight which did not permit the development of my eyeballs. I have what is called *pthisis bulbi*, that's the name of it. They're just like dried up oranges. The doctor knew nothing could be done. He had a partner who was an eye, ear, nose, and throat doctor and they looked and there was nothing. Oh, and my mother didn't drink enough water, she just didn't take care of herself. She worked very hard; she was a farmer's wife. My daddy was a farmer and at that time, they were living together 'til I was nine months old, and then they got divorced.

She had to milk the cows and take care of the horses, and separate the milk, and clean up the milk house, and 'course at the time, there was no prenatal care, so she just didn't have proper care... so she just....I didn't form properly. That's all.

I've just always sung ever since I was twelve years old. First song I sung was something about how to be happy with Jesus. I don't remember what the song was. When I was four years old, even before I went to school, I sang a song about a little candle and I was dressed in a little robe, whatever color candles are I don't know...I think it was green though. I think the robe was green, and I stood up on a table and sang about a little candle for Christmas and, oh, I've just been singing all my life, and so has Baybie.

My uncles and aunts and all of my family were musical people. When I was in school, I'd go to the piano even before I took music lessons and I would find the notes to make it sound like the song did. I just always had the talent for picking out the tune.

I went into religious circles all my life, ever since I was five years old. All my family was religious and we got what we call "converted to Christianity." We embraced Christianity as a way of life so we sang mostly religious songs. If I had my way, I'd sing completely religious songs, but I don't want to be a fanatic, so we just mix 'em up. Whatever Baybie wants, that's what we do. But I've been in religious music ever since I was a little girl — five years old.

We had, oh, a great big stock of the most beautiful cattle you ever saw — it was my grandfather's cattle — and they were good blood 'cause we had a good bull, two good bulls, and, oh, we just sold 'em for one-third less than we bought 'em for, 'cause we lost all our money in '33.

It was all my grandfather's cattle, but I used to ride with him, that gentleman. You know, I said I used to have a little horse. Well, I had a Shetland pony first, and then I had a... and then when my Shetland pony was sold for money why.... Well, my Shetland pony got mean and he used to bite so Grandpa had a big horse and I had Grandpa's horse that he used to use, so I took the horse and I put my Shetland pony out to pasture 'cause he bit me once and I got mad at him so I put him out to pasture and then later on, in 1938 or '39, 1940 it was, I sold him for five dollars.

But I lived in Wichita from the time I was born 'til Grandpa died and then Grandma died.

That gentleman and his wife took my mother to raise — no, they weren't my real grandpa and grandma but — no, they didn't adopt my mother, they just took her to raise. She was not adopted at all, and back in Kansas, there was not any law where you had to be adopted in order to receive money, an inheritance, but back in Illinois there was a law that they had to be adopted. But we moved to Kansas; they moved to Kansas in 1894 so 'course they didn't need to adopt my mother at all 'cause they moved to Kansas in 1894 and so then when I was ten years old, my grandfather, this gentleman, Grandpa Weaver went out in the country.

He had owned a farm ever since they went to Kansas in 1894 and he owned this farm so he went to take care of it himself, 'cause he thought it better 'cause he could get some fresh air — he had trouble with his lungs and with his heart; he needed the fresh air. So we would camp in the summertime ever since I can remember; ever since I was five years old we'd go out camping every summer.

Then when I was ten years old, we'd go out and stay there, oh, weeks on end in the country. We had a hired man and we put a partition on the house so that we lived in one part of the farm house and that hired man lived in the other part. I mostly lived out in the country all my life. I was just around the cattle and around the horses and around the pigs and the sheep. I helped my grandpa perform an autopsy on a sheep once. It died and I held it open while my grandpa examined it. I've had a real farm background you know, kind of a medical background 'cause my grandpa did all his own veterinary work. He had studied medicine at James Millikin University, so Grandpa Weaver was very knowledgeable as far as medicine was concerned. But he got tuberculosis and he couldn't continue so that's why we had to come to Kansas 'cause he had tuberculosis but he got over it when he came to Kansas except that he developed angina pectoris and died in 1933.

My real grandfather was killed in a well. Gas formed in the wall and Grandpa Trimmer was killed. He was a well cleaner, a well driller, and took care of wells and cleaned 'em out and all that. He was an alcoholic and he was drunk and he didn't get out in time, so he died.

Grandma farmed out all her children except the baby, which was Dewey Trimmer; There was Vauna and Norie and Susie and Hazel, which was my mother, and Dewey; and Susie died when she was fourteen years, and then Vauna and Norie and mother and Uncle Dewey got married and raised families, but Aunt Norie died when I was two years old. My Grandma Trimmer was poor and she just kept Uncle Dewey. She was part Indian, so she went down to the reservation down in Southern Illinois somewhere. Then she came back finally and lived with Aunt Vauna 'til she died.

The way that Grandpa Weaver got to know that there were such dire circumstances was that Jake Trimmer and James Weaver played together when they were boys. They knew each other when they were boys. He was quite a wealthy man so he just took my mother. See their two babies had died—Grandpa and Grandma Weaver's two babies had died with cholera and infantum, and one of 'em was stuck to my grandmother and couldn't get out and died in there and that's just the way it was.

When Baybie and I was in summer school in 1941 and '42 in Kansas City, there was a man there by the name of Harold Weisman. He invited me to come to his house for dinner and his folks said, "No, thank you," 'cause I was blind. They didn't want nothin' to do with me, and that was all the boyfriends I had.

Then there was.... We read a notice in a magazine about a deaf person who was blind and deaf, but he could talk and he was advertising for a secretary. Baybie and I are both knowledgeable about typewriters and secretarial work and $200 a month sounded pretty good; so we wrote him a letter and he came to see us. I learned how to talk the language of the deaf and Baybie was busy teaching Braille to the landlady 'cause the landlady was going blind and so Baybie didn't have time to learn the deaf language. That's why she didn't learn it, but I learned it and I tried to talk to him, but we discovered that he wasn't the kind for us, so we took him to the train and sent him back to Chicago.

Baybie and I had lived together in an apartment and she decided she wanted a boarding house. The food didn't satisfy me — the lady was a Seventh Day Adventist and she didn't eat any meat. Now Baybie had a very strong character, now she can adapt to any situation, but not I. I can't or don't, I don't know which. I just couldn't take it, that's all. The food was just horrible and even in 1956 and '57 when we were in New York and in a boarding house...oh, she was a fairly good cook, but I knew that she could cook special food that I 'specially liked, and I asked her to cook 'em and she wouldn't.

It just made me have nervous eats and I'd go out to restaurants and just gorge myself 'til I'd just burst with food — oh, it was a shame. And everything had to be rich. When I cook, I make everything rich, and when the recipe calls for two tablespoons of butter, I put in three, so it's just a shame. You know it's just not good for me and it's a terrible thing.

In 1937, I got me an accordion and I picked it up in my hands and I felt it and I thought wow, what a beauty, and I found C and then I found the major chord of C and then I thought, well, G ought to be up there and I reached up and there was G, reached down, and there was F, and I didn't need to take accordion lessons, but I took seven at five dollars apiece; then I didn't have any more money, so I didn't need any more lessons 'cause I could just pick it out. I knew the piano already from having studied in school and so finally I started playing and that was in 1937. There was a program on the radio called "June Frisbee's Academy," and they had a bunch of accordion players on there and so they used to play music all together. I never was allowed to join the orchestra, but I went to the academy and enrolled for lessons, and they gave me a little bitty accordion with twelve basses. 'Course that wasn't enough for me. I had to have a great big 48 basses. Now I got given a 120, which is more my size. Yes, it's got all the keys on it, you know, and all the chords and everything. And I can play the organ, any kind of organ, after examining it.

But, oh, I can play an organ, a piano, accordion and I s'pose I can play a xylophone if I just practiced 'cause it's just got piano keys like, and you just hit it with hammers and I can play a little on the violin, but I squeak 'cause I haven't learned to keep off the bridge, and I can play a harmonica and I can play a melodica, and I think I can play a guitar with a bar on it 'cause I did once a long time ago. When I was about eleven or twelve years old, somebody gave me a guitar with a bar and I could make chords with it. I forgot how, but I think I could pick it up again if I tried. But I love to just fool around with instruments. I love to take just take 'em in my hands and just look at 'em forever, and just feel 'em and experiment, you know. And oh yes, the autoharp. I can play that and I can tune it too. It takes me forever, but I can do it, and I don't think there isn't an instrument that I wouldn't tackle; I would tackle any kind of instrument. But I haven't got any teeth and so I don't think I could play a trumpet. I love music, I just... music is my life and I love music.

End of Virginia Brown reel

So anyway, Virginia and I got into this Bible conference when I was about twenty-seven, and there was a girl there, a young girl; she was a college representative. She said, "Why don't you girls come to college?" I said, "My God, we don't have any money". She said, "Come by faith." "All right," I said, "We will." I was eager to have more Bible training anyway because I knew the Lord had definitely called me to preach, and I knew that I had better get on with it. And so we did go a year to this Bible college in Iowa, and I worked my way in the kitchen. I'd peel potatoes, wash dishes and things like that. I worked my way through college.

During the year, Virginia... well, she's just naturally obstructive ... they threatened to send us both home. Virginia says, "Well, I'll go home", but she didn't. I mean she offered to but she didn't. They let us finish the year. So, as a consequence, I only got a year where I could have maybe had several more.

So then after college was over, why we, I decided to live in Wichita 'cause, like I said, I didn't see any point in Buzz and I living together really 'cause Buzz, you know, he'd go out with other women and that was all right. I didn't blame him for that; I was glad, you know, that he could get his sex life satisfied; of course I don't suppose that he was a flaming torch, but still, you know he had something which was more than I did. I was dead. I had nothing.... So then we (Virginia and I) started living together in Wichita. We had a little apartment. We've lived together off and on 'til we moved to New York.

Brother Taylor — he was a real old minister in Wichita — he thought he would take us girls to a revival meeting that he was going to have in Tulsa, Oklahoma. We came on the bus — it wasn't any kind of sex deal or anything — and he was the preacher and we were gonna sing the songs. He put us up at an uncle or a brother of his or his wife. We stayed there and he stayed in his trailer. He had a little trailer home like I said; it was all up and up. But it didn't work out too well.

Brother Taylor, he used to have street meetings every Saturday night in Wichita. He had a permit and 'course he'd preach and we'd sing. I thought that was great; 'course he'd take up an offering and 'course he'd keep two thirds of it and we'd get one third of the money. So we did this for a long, long time, and got the brilliant idea, why goodness, why don't we do this ourselves?

So finally, well I said we'd stick to it, 'cause he had awful high blood pressure and he was a sick man and we knew he couldn't last too much longer, you know, 'cause he was just in awful shape. So when he died, I mean I did cry 'cause he had been awful good to us girls and he had faith in us and no one else did. He'd taken us to that revival meeting and gotten the shitty end of the stick, you know, as the world would say.

So after he died, I said to myself, "So all right, I'm gonna get myself a permit." I went down to the police station and I said I'd like to apply for a permit for street work. I said I had a license. Oh, yes, and in Udall, Kansas, I had got a license, a preacher's license from the Church of the Nazarene 'cause they heard me preach and they said, certainly I could have a license to preach; it was called a "local license," in other words, licensed by the local church.

As I progressed I could have gotten my next license, which would have been a district license, which would be licensed by the district church you know a combination of the whole district, they said I could have gone on and got ordained in the Church of the Nazarene; but then Virginia up and joined the Wesleyan Methodist Church, and I, like a stupid, crazy, loyal fool, went and joined the church with her and, of course, I lost my license.... That was the second big mistake of my lifetime.

So Virginia and I joined this Wesleyan Methodist Church and I got an exhorter's license, which is way down at the bottom. I said, "Look, I already have my preacher's license from the Church of the Nazarene." He says, "Well, I believe in you starting at the bottom."

And oh, I was just sick. I thought, "My goodness, I've already got my preacher's license," and he says "We'll see how you get along." Well, Virginia and I we just scrapped and fought and scrapped and fought and finally I says, "Look, I don't want to be a preacher anyway." I said, "I don't think I'm worthy to be 'cause I cannot get along with this person, and you know, if you're gonna be a preacher, you gotta get along with people," and I says, "You gonna profess to be a preacher and a Christian," I said, "You gotta quit cussin' around." Oh, I was cursing and everything; I was having an awful time and I just about lost my whole faith in God through the whole process.

I was about twenty-eight after we came back from college, after we'd made a miserable failure there and we'd made a miserable failure at that revival meeting in Oklahoma. And we made a miserable failure every time — I mean, not every time — we'd get up to give a performance but I never knew when it was gonna break loose.

Before Brother Taylor died, he was in the meeting one night and I was gonna give up my license. He said, "Oh sister, don't do that", he said, "Don't give up your license, you're all right." You know, he tried to encourage me. I said, "Im not all right, Brother Taylor," and then Brother Smith, the minister of the church, said, "If she isn't worthy, why then they'll take her license." I mean he was very strict. I said, "You can have it." So I turned it in, my exhorter's license. So then I didn't do any more preaching for some time.

After this, Brother Taylor died, why, I went and got my permit again and still kept preaching on the streets, even though I turned in my license. I thought, oh well, St. Peter did. I still had my Nazarene, yes. I still did have that license, and I clung to that and in all my moving around I finally lost it.

We did this street work in Wichita, Kansas, beginning in 1946, and then they advertised in a national Braille magazine about the Gospel Association for the Blind in New York City. And of course we thought it was a national thing because it was advertised in this magazine that went all over the country. So Virginia and I said, "Well, let's go to New York and see if we can help this Dr. Montanus."

Oh, I had my doubts, you know. I mean, I knew that Ginger... I was afraid she'd obstruct it, but you know I just didn't want it to be so. I thought, "Well, each time, you know, each opportunity we'd have," I'd think, "well, surely she's learned her lesson, you know, surely we'll learn." And I just wanted that to be true.

The trip was fun for us. We had to change busses a few times so I kept our paper folded up in my dress pocket to show our routes and times so bus people could help us and be sure we got on the right bus. We had a story in case anyone asked us why two young girls was travelin' alone. We concocted that we was cousins and that our folks had died in a fire and we was going to New York to stay with an aunt of ours that had a home there. 'Course, bein' blind it's impossible to tell how peoples is reading what we's sayin', but we could tell somewhat by their questions afterwards. We always feared that someone askin' would call the police or some agency and turn us in, but we arrived three days later in New York City without any troubles along the way. I only wish I could have seen what was out those windows as we passed by half the country.

Blind folks have ways of understanding things that are different from sighted folks. The big words I learned at the school for the blind were proprioception and reverberation. I could tell easily when I was in a big space or a small space by the reverberation of sounds inside the space. They explained to us that the time a sound takes to go from where it started to a wall or ceiling, bounce off, and come back to the blind person's ear helps 'em perceive how big the space is. I guess the biggest indoor spaces I'd been in was churches. I learned that choirs always sound better in big spaces 'cause their singin' gets filled out by reverberation, which is just fast echoes.

Ginger and I knew right away we was in the biggest space we'd ever been in after we climbed off that bus and went through the doors into the bus station in New York City. We could hear hundreds a folks talkin' all at once and cups clattering and luggage being dragged across the floor. I tried to imagine how big the space was. The floor was like stone so all the noise kept bouncing around forever in there.

We knew we needed a place to stay, but was afraid to ask. We'd heard of Traveler's Aid Societies, but feared they might remand two young blind women to the authorities. We both needed a bathroom and a man aimed us in the right direction. He must a thought he was being funny 'cause he sent us into the men's room where we was politely asked to leave by an understanding man who, I think, was a cleaner in there. He had a Negro way of speaking. He showed us the lady's room which was next door. I never seen what was funny about people doing those jokes on blind people, but some people think things is funny that ain't.

I then asked a stranger where the street door was and, oh, we musta looked funny. We had our first experience with rotating doors. We always walked close on one another and we both walked into one section. Sometimes Ginger would just fold up her Hoover stick and hold on the back of my dress. I pushed on the door and the door behind us broke Ginger's stick when it closed up behind her. We'd never seen a door that closed behind you so we just stood there in that tiny space with our one valise, not knowing what to do. We was trapped. Then the door began to rotate when someone came in behind us, and that rear door just swept us out onto the big sidewalks of New York City.

What a racket! .... Cars and trucks and car horns tootin' and people talkin' everywhere. Cigarette smoke everywhere and we heard some people talking in a way we didn't understand. We knew there was other languages people spoke. But we'd never heard 'em bein' spoken. That was the first things we learned in New York. Even some people who did speak English spoke it in a way we never heard and it was hard at first to follow 'em, even though they was using the same words and all.

I felt on Ginger's broken stick and half of it was missing so we left it near a street light 'cause we didn't know they had garbage cans right on the street. I used my stick and Ginger held on the back of my dress. 'Course, I had to carry the valise, 'cause I was bigger than Ginger but I didn't mind.

I'd been taught in Kansas City to walk on a city street and I still had that learnin'. 'Course, Ginger hadn't ever seen what we was hearin' but told me just the same what was what around us. She's like that. We had to stay close on one another just to hear ourselves. No pictures came up for me of what she was sayin'. But at least Ginger knew to tell what she thought was dangerous.

We crossed several streets with some help from folks and found a quiet corner. I set down my valise and we just then and there decided we'd sing a song together to make us feel less lonely in such a big city. We sang *I Saw the Light* and half way through a man came up and put a quarter in my hand. I wasn't holding out my hand. He just took it like he was going to shake my hand, opened it up and set a quarter on my palm. I thanked him while Ginger carried the hymn and I put the quarter in my pocket with our bus paper.

I saw the light, I saw the light
No more darkness, no more night
Now I'm so happy, no sorrow in sight
Praise the Lord, I saw the light

I wandered so aimless, my heart filled with sin
I wouldn't let my dear Savior in
Then Jesus came like a stranger in the night
Praise the Lord, I saw the light

I saw the light, I saw the light
No more darkness, no more night
Now I'm so happy, no sorrow in sight
Praise the Lord, I saw the light

Just like a blind man I wandered alone
Worries and fears, I claimed for my own
Then like the blind man that God gave back his sight
Praise the Lord, I saw the light

I saw the light, I saw the light
No more darkness, no more night
Now I'm so happy, no sorrow in sight
Praise the Lord, I saw the light

I was a fool to wander and stray
Straight is the gate and narrow the way
Now I have traded the wrong for the right
Praise the Lord, I saw the light

I saw the light, I saw the light
No more darkness, no more night
Now I'm so happy, no sorrow in sight
Praise the Lord, I saw the light

We felt like God had visited us and I kept my hand open a bit and sure enough folks put in some coins while we was singin'. That inspired me to sing "Precious Lord, Take My Hand" and the coins just kept comin' our way.

Precious Lord, take my hand
Lead me on, let me stand

I am tired, I am weak, I am worn
Through the storm, through the night
Lead me on to the light
Take my hand precious Lord, lead me home

When my way grows drear
Precious Lord linger near
When my life is almost gone
Hear my cry, hear my call
Hold my hand lest I fall
Take my hand precious Lord, lead me home

When the darkness appears
And the night draws near
And the day is past and gone
At the river I stand
Guide my feet, hold my hand
Take my hand precious Lord, lead me home

Precious Lord, take my hand
Lead me on, let me stand
I'm tired, I'm weak, I'm alone
Through the storm, through the night
Lead me on to the light
Take my hand precious Lord, lead me home

The Lord must've been with these two blind girls in the big city, 'cause after another hour of singing we had almost three dollars in coins.

It's hard for a sighted person to fathom the din of a big city on two scared blind girls from Kansas. In a world of brash sounds roaring up on you from every direction and odors creeping slowly in with no pictures in your head, we couldn't make any sense of the world around us. At home, we was used to hearing a car or one kid on a bike or an old man muttering to himself as he passed by and we could have a plan in our heads but when they's all rushin' in on you like in the city, we couldn't separate out the meaningful sounds from the general din and know what to pay attention to or be warned on. The sounds and smells kept us fearful and made us more tired from always trying to sort it and make some sense of it. Virginia often says things right and she said to me it was like going out on a dance floor with your beau and then having twenty dance bands all start to play a different tune at once. Ya wouldn't know whether to jitterbug, shimmy, Lindy hop, or Charleston.

Ginger wanted to use our three dollars to buy a meal. She was always hungry it seemed, but I was thinking on where we'd sleep that night.

After about an hour of singin', we was thirsty and asked someone where we could get a drink of water or a lemonade. Funny, but we was standing in front of a soda fountain and she pointed us inside. We was told you had to buy something to sit down so Ginger and I each just spent ten cents on a lemonade. We drank 'em slowly so's we have a place to sit for a minute after standing so long on the sidewalk. After we was refreshed, we asked the soda jerk where there was a cheap hotel. He was a callous youth and laughed at us, saying they're everywhere. I picked up our valise and we left. I didn't know which direction we was walking. We just kept walking and at one intersection a woman asked if she could help us. She must a known that we didn't know where we was headed. The first few nights was hard. Again, we didn't have no place to sleep and it was getting cooler, like fall was comin' early. We both forgot we'd traveled north and it was bound to be colder sooner. It was also hard because we was still young and women's always targets.

The next day we sang on the corner of 42d Street and 8th avenue right near where the bus landed us on the first day, but we soon learned it was just too noisy there and everybody was in a hurry and din't have time to listen to two girls singin' Jesus songs at the top of their lungs to be heard above the trucks and busses.

At the end of that first day on our own, we was tired and hoarse from singing too loud. Since the bus terminal was open all night, we slept in there on a bench and took turns being awake so one of us could say we was waitin' on a bus. I could tell from the echo of the public address announcer's voice callin' busses how big it was in there and Ginger and I imagined it was like an enclosed city where lots of people lived all night and day. It was too noisy to sleep and whichever one of us it was's turn to sleep didn't get no rest. The public address was announcing bus departures or arrivals every few minutes and it had to be turned up real loud to get through the din of all the people talking and shufflin' about. I'd drift off, but my mind never could turn off all the hearin'. It was a half sleep, like one gets sometime falling asleep in church but remember the sermon.

The next morning, we was both tired.

All night creepy men came up and asked us if we needed any help or offered to take us to a place where we could have a warm bed. We was polite, but firm that we weren't leavin' that bench. We both knew what these creeps wanted. Oh yah, we'd get a nice warm bed and all, but surprise,... they'd be in it. Besides we had our bearings on where the bathroom was. But after the first night in the bus station, we knew not to spend another night there.

When morning came and we bought a roll and some coffee at the coffee stand, we talked on how we wouldn't spend another night in the terminal.

We learned on the street that rich folks lived further north in the city and we was advised by a kindly man to go up where the rich people stores was on Fifth Avenue and 57th Street. Well, that lasted about half an hour 'cause we was chased away by a policeman who told us that begging was illegal and he didn't want to hear my explanation about how we was workin' women and all. He told us in no uncertain terms to get out of his sight or he'd call for the paddy wagon and have arrested.

Looking back on it after all these years I realize we had picked a section of town that was too rich. We was near the Plaza and Tiffany's and the Savoy Plaza. Rich people don't like being reminded about poor folks even though many of 'em was once. I suppose that's why. It's painful to remember where they come from.

Anyways, Ginger and I learned that the very rich ain't that generous in spite of having more to give. It's often those with least to give that's the most generous, like they're not so far away from their own troubles as to have forgotten what hardship's like. So we decided to move further east and that's how we ended up outside of Bloomingdale's on 59th Street ... Been there ever since.

Don't get me wrong, mostly rich people shop at Bloomingdale's, but most of our pay comes from people walking up and down Third Avenue or Lex., wherever we happen to be singing that day. We haven't tried all over the city, but we always do well here, especially in winter.

But I'm gettin' ahead a' myself again. So, after many nights on the street, sleeping in doorways and on subway grates and one scary night in Central Park, we finally got help from a friendly policeman on Lexington who never bothered us. In fact he'd once asked us to sing one or two of his favorite songs which we obliged, and he'd toss a few quarters in my cup. It was funny 'cause he took out his ticket pad for writing up cars and he wrote down the name of the city agency that would help us find a place to live. He handed the ticket to me and said, "This place will.... Oh me, you all can't read that 'cause you're blind. I'm not very smart."

He was a young man, probably not much older than we was. He apologized and said he felt stupid writing us an address. But Ginger and I made him feel good about it and we all had a good laugh on it. I told him that if he said the street address and name of the place I could remember it easily. You see blind folks have to have a better memory than sighted folks 'cause they have so much they have to remember.

The next day we went to the place. It was a big office and we had a long wait until our names were called. We lost half a day's pay sitting on them benches waiting to be called up for giving help. After a lot of back and forth, it seemed we was disabled because of our being blind and all and qualified for "emergency placement" as the man said. We was told where to go and given a piece of paper to give to the person at that address and we would be given emergency shelter for as long as we needed it.

When the nice man asked what we did for a living, I told him we were street singers. "Vaudeville?" he asked. I told him no, that we mostly sang old hymns and radio tunes, but that we was always learning more songs and I asked him if he would like us to sing him a song. He said he would someday, but not now.

We left the big office and walked all the way to the address he gave us on West 49th Street. It seemed like several miles. Inside, I gave the paper to the man at the desk. He took a bunch of keys and we rode up an elevator to the fourth floor where he unlocked a room and told us that that was our place to be. He said the bathroom was down the hall and that inside our room we'd find a key that would unlock the bathroom door, but always to knock before going in, as the rooms on this floor all shared the bathroom. He then left.

The room smelled funny. We palpated around and found there was a single bed and a dresser and a sink with cold running water. I opened the window and we agreed that next time we bought some things, we'd get some pine soap and give the place a thorough going over. Well after all these years, it's still my home today and I've come to like it.

I got acquainted with this Woodrow Wilson, you know, "Woody." We met him in a restaurant in about 1957; we've known him a long time. I had moved into my room at the Markwell and we went in to eat at a little place called the Oasis, which doesn't even exist anymore.

It was pouring down rain and this Markwell Hotel was very good to blind streetworkers, you know. There was a lot of blind streetworkers lived in that hotel. We went to the desk and, when we finally decided to actually get down to business and work on the street, and we were talking, and I said, "We don't have any cup," the manager heard me and he says, "I have a cup you can have." By God, he gave me a cup!! I about flipped.

Oh, I laugh to think on it today and I was so thrilled! And I says, "Oh, thank you!" The thought that he would aid me and abet me to panhandle! Now that tickled me to death!! He knew it was against the law. It was the very same day and he also gave Virginia a cup, two cups! There's two of you, you'll need two cups. Oh wow, he wanted to be sure he got his rent. That was the only way.

We had got off the welfare in the meantime because someone had told that we were working on the street and they asked us how much we made and I says, "It's none of your business!" I said, "We make different amounts. It would be very hard to tell you how much we make," I said, "Some days we make such and such and some days we make such and such else." And I said, "It's according to when it rains; there's nothing regular about it. We just do the best we can."

And he said, "Well, you can't work on the street and stay on welfare," (that was at that time), so they took the welfare away from us. We had to really get into earnest for sure.

Well, as I was saying...don't I jump around though? We went into this Oasis Restaurant and it started pouring down rain that day we got our cups. I said, "Well, well, well."

So we went in there, you know, to get a little sandwich and — why every situation that comes up, why I always have a song to fit it. So I sung, "Just a-singing in the rain," and of course there was a song, you know, and this Woodrow Wilson, he was behind the counter; he says, "Just a-walking in the rain, getting soaking wet, no money in my cup, they're gonna starve me yet."

And I thought, "What in the world?"

I says, "Oh, you know about streetworkers?"

And he says, "That's right."

I says, "That's a cute song!" I says, "That's a cute version to it." And then Virginia and I start singing it right in the restaurant. 'Course he was the manager of the restaurant, so we start singing, "Walking in the rain, getting soaking wet, no money in the cup," and Virginia put the alto to it, you know. And we were singing in there so he helped us. He helped me to locate several spots to work, you know. He told me different places where I could go to work. And of course I wasn't, you know, I couldn't see and I wasn't too familiar with all the spots in Manhattan. And he gave me several spots to work.

Anyways, Virginia and me found our way to the Thanksgiving dinner of the Gospel Association for the Blind and 'course they introduced us and they said they had a couple here from Kansas and we joined an amateur contest. They had a little amateur contest and we sang our songs; we sang a couple of songs. That was it; they wanted us to work for 'em. And so they put us to work out on the street in this crazy deal where they got two-thirds of it and we got a third. They had about eight donation boxes altogether. They did at that time, eight different boxes with two people on a box. So we worked for them for about three months.

After they let us go, they said, "Look, we'll give you money to go back to Kansas," and I told Virginia, "Let's take 'em up on it," and Virginia said, "No," 'cause she kept thinking they'd hire us back. So Virginia wouldn't hear of it, I was ready to just pack it in and go on back to Kansas. I guess the Lord just didn't want us to, 'cause Virginia wouldn't hear of it.

I really did like New York. I didn't want to go back to Kansas but I thought, what the heck, might as well, nothing here anymore. You know.

So Montanus said, "Did you girls decide to go back to Kansas?" I said, "No." He said, "Why?" I said, "We happen to like New York." And he said, "Well, I don't know what you like about it."

I said, "Well, why do you stay here then?" I said, "We happen to love New York and we're stayin'!"

He said, "Well, don't work on the street. If we see you doing it we'll call the police."

I said, "Police, here we come!"

Well, you see they still had their street solicitors and they knew that we were quite capable of taking money away from them.

So Virginia wouldn't work on the street 'cause she was afraid that Montanus would catch her. I said, "So what?" I said, "What can he do?"

We had about eleven hundred dollars that we had saved, you know, between us and we used it all up. And we got where we couldn't pay our rent, and I said, "Now look, Ginger, we're gonna have to start working, that's all there is to it."

We finally got on welfare, and they gave us a little old piddly $32, well, $64 a month, $32 every two weeks. And I said, "My God, I can't live like this."

So finally, some of the Christians persuaded Ginger she ought to be out singing for the Lord, and so we started working on the street again, but she wouldn't go out except at night, you know, 'cause she was afraid Ralph would catch her. And we had to do all our work in Times Square in the middle of the night — oh, and such a life I don't even want to think about it.... Those times, I'm telling you, from 1954 on was just, oh, they were torture.

One day on the street, we met a nice lady. Her voice was kindly and I risked telling her the truth, that we'd come to New York City from Kansas to make our way singing to folks. She asked if we ever heard of the Lighthouse, and we pretended we hadn't. She explained that it was special for blind people and helped them get started and have a place to live and learn how to work and all. It sounded good to us and we had no other plan.

The kindly lady hailed a taxi and told the driver where to take us. I told her we didn't have enough money to pay 'cause I couldn't see that she had already paid the driver. She pressed a dollar into each of our hands and wished us well.

I sat back on that leather seat and them sobs come at me again. To this day, I don't know what it is about a person's kindness towards me that sets me to sobbin' so. I should be happy when folks is kind, but I just start cryin', still do to this day.

We didn't drive far. The Lighthouse must have been pretty close to where we was singin' 'cause the driver told us we was there. He knew we were blind so he offered to walk us to the door, another kindness. I began to wonder if everyone in the big city was kind, but I soon learned different.

The lady who greeted us inside was very nice she asked us how old we was and we had both agreed to lie about our age so as not to be remanded. Lord knows why; we was middle age women by then.

We told her we was older than we was. We must a looked that 'cause she didn't question it. She called someone on the phone and invited us to sit on a couch until that someone came. The lady who came was very nice, she said she would be asking us a lot of questions and then she could figure out how best to help us.

I told her we was fine on our own and didn't need a place to stay but we had no money yet, as we had just started working.

She went on about all the things the Lighthouse did for blind folks and how they could help us and all. I explained that I had been to a school for the blind, could read Braille and could take pretty good care of myself. She asked how we were planning to support ourselves and I told her singing and that someday we hoped to be on the radio like Una Mae. She said she never heard tell of Una Mae, but that they had a music school and could teach us how to play instruments and all.

I think it may have been getting near her quitting time 'cause she suggested we spend the night and that we continue making a plan in the morning. She called someone else who showed us to a room in the building up a flight of stairs and where the bath was and all.

Ginger and I took turns having a long bath, since there didn't seem to be a lot of people in the Lighthouse shelter that night. I let Ginger go first then I added some more hot water and climbed into the big tub.

Lyin' in a warm tub always put me in a mind of my Anna and I got real sad. I counted how old she'd be now and remembered that she'd be a young woman. I asked the Lord to quell my feelings of anger, but sometimes it just felt like the Lord wasn't there, like when Mr. Desmets was havin' his carnal spells on me. I vowed again that someday I would find Anna and we'd be united.

I musta fell asleep in the tub 'cause I heard someone knocking on the door that I had locked. Lucky, it was Ginger. I got up and out and dried off and went back to our little room. There was two cots and Ginger and me slept like newborns.

Someone had to wake us up the next morning and we'd missed the breakfast meal, but another lady than the one who talked with us the night before brought us some cold buttered toast to eat and glasses of milk. We was grateful for her kindness but began to feel a bit like we was being remanded and needed to escape.

She asked a lot of nosey questions that made us both nervous, on where was we livin', how we was earnin' our keep, like she thought we might be floozies or something. Anyway, the woman condescended to us and said that being a mendicant was not a way to live. I didn't know the word "mendicant" and asked her what it meant. She explained that it was a polite word for a street beggar. Then I knew not to trust her politeness and her condescending tone. I had no desire to try and explain to her that Virginia and I work hard for our living, small as it is.

Finally, after telling all the Lighthouse could do for us, she asked if we had any questions. Ginger spoke up and asked how long we could just sleep there and the woman said that they could provide emergency shelter for up to three days and then folks had to have a life plan. We didn't know what a life plan was, but it sounded like we'd have to agree to something we didn't know.

She went on, telling how they had classes in Braille and crafts we could learn but we would have to stop being mendicants. I let her know in no uncertain terms that I read Braille and had learned crafts at the School for the Blind in Kansas. My craft, I explained, was not tatting doilies or making baskets, but singing in public places.

We allowed as we'd like to think on it and see to our options, but that we would meet with her again on the third day to work out our "life plan." This seemed to satisfy her and I got up and left.

I waited on the street for Virginia, but she didn't come out right away. I was sensing inside that she liked the sound of what the woman was saying, especially the craft room part and the emergency sleeping quarters and all the music courses. Virginia is an accomplished musician and plays a lot of instruments like the piano we have in our little church.

The next day we was both at work on time and neither of us talked about the visit to the Lighthouse again. It still makes me mad as hell when I think about that woman talking down to us like that. I did take my name "Baybie" there though, and since our visit there, I've always been the Reverend Baybie Hoover. I suppose there's always some grateful in our adversities.

I think the thing that was most hard getting used to in New York was the constant racket. There was noise every second of the day, even when you was sleepin'. I'd hear trucks slammin' on their brakes, taxis blowin' their horns, people yellin' at one another. 'Course I was used to quiet out in Kansas where the only night sounds you heard was the 'casional sound of a bird, a hoot owl, or geese honkin' overhead, or maybe a tractor in the spring or fall whining away in the far distance, or a train bullin' through the cornfields hauling its freight and whistle-blowin' at the crossings. Each sound had meaning in the landscape and you could know it and see it in your mind's eye. It would get me imagin' on people or birds goin' places, doin' things. 'Course, being with Anna at the School for the Blind, she'd tell what things looked like from her sighted time... trains and birds and such so I could image something when I heard the sound. Hearin' tell about it ain't like bein' sighted but it's as good as I got and I could see something in my mind.

Sometimes Anna'd have me touch on things in our room to get a feeling for what something felt like. Like the time we was in the reception area and she had me touch a fur coat hanging on a peg that she'd smelled hanging there. She told me that's what some animals felt like, and 'course, later, I'd touched the farm animals at the Desmets'.

It's hard sometimes when you're blind, 'cause you don't know what or where you're touching something and if you might get bit or hurt. I loved the feeling of the two cows at the Desmets. They had a smooth warm feel and you could sometimes feel the organs inside 'em workin' away makin' milk and digestin' hay and whatever they do.

Now just listen to me talkin' about what goes on inside a cow. Don't I beat all sometimes?

If I know'd I was alone when gathering eggs at night, I'd sometimes pick up the broody hen and just hold her in my arms like a baby. She was in the second nest from the left in the top row. I could never catch one during the day when they was scrabblin' about the yard 'cause I didn't know where they were 'cept by the sound of their gabblin' and Mrs. Desmets might get after me for disturbin' her brood. But at night when it was dark, they'd let you pick 'em up and just hold 'em. That broody hen was so warm and soft in the feathers on her belly, I could have just sat down right there in that henhouse and held her all night. She'd make funny little noises when I'd stroke the back of her head where the rufflin' feathers are. I guess I just like motherin' things.

Anyway I was talking about noise, not touchin' things. It took me weeks to get used to that racket. I don't think Virginia ever did. I worried a lot that Ginger just couldn't let herself feel things what troubled her, bottlin' 'em up inside, makin' her sick sometimes. Later on Ginger came into doing things that wasn't rational, but I've always been there to help her find her way back. I learned in my long years with Ginger that you can only help someone so much before they have to take over and do their own healin', with or without the Lord's help.

Unless you know what it's like to be blind, you can't imagine it. At least with smell, one smell is above the others and you only worry about that smell. Most smells like car smoke you can't do anything about. The smell of dog poop or garbage cans puts you on awares to be careful where you're walking. Good food smells, like comes out of the deli bakeries or a restaurant makes you hungry. But usually you're figurin' on just one smell.

With sounds, though, it's like being flooded. If you're walkin' with your stick, you hear the traffic on one side of you and you hear the people comin' towards you. You hear music comin' out of a record store. You hear sirens about trouble. Sometimes you hear people tryin' to sell you something. People ask if you need help and it's all at once like a thousand messages comin' at you and you have to parse each one out and think on what it means. Are you walking right? Are you too close to the curb? Are people going to walk into you? Is someone somewhere getting hurt? Why is that man running? Is there danger?

And it never ends. You lie in bed at night and you hear the trucks loading and unloading. Where I live there's a lot of freight and you hear trucks coming and going all night long and men shouting to one another about what they's unloading and where they's gonna put it or sometimes about nothin'. I hear a woman scream and worry what's happening to her and hope it ain't what happened to me, even though I didn't scream 'cause there wasn't no one to hear a girl screamin' in the empty fields of Kansas.

It's like when you turn the tuning dial on a radio too fast and hear all those sounds too fast to know what any one is.

I think it was the city noise that made Virginia unstable. I don't like judgin' on my friend, but Virginia hasn't been herself since we got here. She lives by herself somewhere downtown and don't ever tell me where. She wants to be alone and that's okay with me, 'cause I like living alone too, though it's easier in a big city to live with someone so you don't have to do all your chores alone and you have someone to talk to. Every day I worry whether she'll show up for work, but she does every day; she has for all these years.

I worry she has no bathroom place 'cause I don't think she bathes and she smells bad in the summer. Hard enough for kindly folks to approach a blind person anyway... seems like they'se afraid they'll catch it so it's important to act normal and to smell and look clean. We sing about cleanliness and godliness, but I don't think it rubs off on Ginger. I worry about her being all secretive, but I don't ask anymore, 'cause she just don't answer questions she don't like. Kind of like we're more business partners than friends now, but that's okay because we both make a good enough living at our job.

Ginger told me once that most people believe that all blind people got that way from sex diseases and that's why they don't like to be anywhere near a blind person for fear of catchin' their disease and going blind themselves. I did hear tell that some sex diseases can cause blindness, but then so do drunken doctors.

I learned early on when singin' on the street that you have to hold your tin cup far away from yourself 'cause people, for whatever reasons, still have trouble approaching a street singer. It's hard holding that cup out all day, but I got used to it and grew a muscle for it.

Ginger won't do it and when I talked about it with her, she just said, "I don't care, they'll pay what they pay. I can't hold that cup out all day and play the accordion, can't be." She had a point. She pins her cup to her chest and some people do put money in, but they don't like to get that close so usually they put the money in my cup.

Don't matter since we split up everything at the end of the day anyways. Ginger can be difficult though. I'd be difficult if I'd been through her travails though she never talks about 'em so I never did know the whole story. Maybe she'll tell it to you if you ask her.

Virginia stayed with me for the first few months and tried to share a single bed, which was hard for me because she didn't practice proper hygiene. Also, we'd both lost our girlish slimness.

I'd ask her to bathe, but she said she didn't believe the lock on the bathroom door was strong enough to prevent someone from coming in on her while she was in the tub. I know something happened to her, but she just chose to keep it close. She didn't even feel comfortable going into the bathroom down there and, at night if she had to pee, she'd pee in an old saucepan she kept for that purpose and then she'd empty it like a chamber pot in the morning.

She never did sleep well either and tossed and turned a lot in the bed which, 'course, kept me awake. Even as young girls, we needed our sleep 'cause singin' long hours on the street is hard work and we'd have to walk at almost forty blocks just to get to work until we was given subway passes by the public welfare people who got us our room.

Ginger and I didn't fight. Oh, she had it in her, but we just had a bargain that we wouldn't argue on things. We'd just let 'em be.

But Ginger's lack of cleanliness soon made it impossible for me. We got lice and God knows what other critters took up residence on her. I was always a clean person and always saw to takin' care not to have any odor or dirt on me. I cut my hair and cleaned and trimmed my nails regular. Poor Ginger just let herself go, always making the excuse that she didn't like to have to be naked or be in a bathroom.

I offered to fill the pitcher and she could wash in the room, but after we'd finish workin' and have something to eat, Ginger'd just pull off her outer clothes and climb into bed. We only got clean sheets every two weeks and I hated being that dirty.

Ginger was hard to get to know. Seemed like she had bad stuff bottled up inside her, but she didn't like talkin' on it much. She wasn't like me. I love to talk once I trust someone 'cause I learned that sharin' lowers the weight of a pain or hurt. Even knowin' Ginger as long as I do today, I don't think she can trust anyone 'cept in the present. Even now, she questions me sometimes like I didn't share our earnings right or I took more of the food then I gave to her or something like that and we been singing together for twenty years.

We finally had it out. Ginger said nothing and after work she didn't come home with me.

That night I felt terrible and prayed to God she was okay. I worried on something happening to her and knew it would be my fault. But the next day she was at our singing spot even before I was. She didn't say anything about our set-to, so I didn't, and it was like it never happened, and she never came back to that room. I knew then not to ask her if she had a place 'cause I knew she would simply pretend like she didn't hear me. She's strange that way on her privacy.

Life went on well for us both. We'd stop for lunch and usually get a hot dog at the *Papaya King* down the street and Mercedes, the counter woman, always put a little extra something on our plates. Back then we could get a hot dog for a quarter. She explained that as long as she rang all her sales in the register, the boss never accounted for what she put on the plate. She was real nice. She said she was from a country called Puerto Rico, where a lot of New York people came from, and we got used to how they talked so we would know when we were talking with someone from Puerto Rico.

I'd keep to myself at my house but the nice barber near my entrance would always yell a friendly "Hello, Baybie" to me if he saw me coming or going. He's the man who found me my chair I like so much.

One day when he didn't have any customers and was chatting me, he told me he had a friend who was the maitre d' at a small Italian family restaurant four blocks north on 20th Street. He told me if I went there and mentioned his name that Aldo would have some food for Ginger and me so I stopped there on my way home and went in the front door and asked for Aldo. The man I asked was Aldo and, like Eddy told, he was very nice when he heard I was a friend of Eddy's. He told me to knock on the back door in the alley on the left just beyond the garbage cans and that he would see to it that there was small box for me when we came home from work.

I got Ginger to come with me the next night and we did as Aldo had suggested and sure enough, someone in the kitchen unlocked the door and handed us a box about the size of a shoe box.

The smells coming out of that kitchen were so good. I can smell different kinds of foods and the smells told me that this was an Italian restaurant. Usually, the box would contain leftovers from the lunch servings, usually some lasagna or ravioli in a box lined with wax paper. There'd be some soft rolls and a few pats of butter as well.

It was such a treat after a long day to have a fully cooked meal and it didn't cost us a thing. It was against the rules to cook in your room, though from the smells I expect some people in the welfare house did. You wasn't allowed to use immersion heaters or cookplates or electric irons for fear of fire in the wiring. There was one light bulb in the ceiling which 'course I never turned on and then there was a place to plug a radio or a clock into. I didn't have a radio and couldn't read a clock so I guess I didn't use much electricity.

I have a radio now, but I never turn it on 'cause there's nothin' I want to hear. The radio preacher shows don't reach the big city and besides their music today ain't what I'm used to. I was talking about food though — don't I just circle around in my thoughts!

So every night, I'd stop and knock on that door and every night, there'd be a little treat for me. After a few days, Ginger stopped coming. It was way out of her way 'cause the subway she took back to where she was livin' went down toward the Lower East Side under Lexington Avenue where we sang and coming to Aldo's was too far out of her way. I s'pect she didn't like Italian food cause she said it gave her sour stomach. Well it gave me sour stomach too, but I didn't care. I loved it and I'd be so hungry after working all day.

I began listening again to radio when Eddy gave me the old one in his barber shop. It was a tube radio and I loved laying my hands on it just to warm 'em up. Eddy's father also worked in the barber shop. He loved the Brooklyn Dodgers and would always have his radio on when they was playin'. Eddy told that when the Dodgers left Brooklyn, his father unplugged the radio and never turned it on again. It just collected dust until the day Eddy offered it to me.

I recollected all those days out on the Kansas prairie listening to radio preachers from Texarkana. At first, I had trouble findin' them. Luckily, I only listened at night. For some reason the number of stations on the dial doubled late at night. Lots of 'em's on the air all day but their waves only seemed to reach New York late at night.

At first, I listened every night until late. The radio would take me home and the city noises would seem to disappear. Oh, I had my favorite preachers, but mostly I liked the singin'.

There was a station in Grand Prairie, Texas, I 'specially liked, they had a little girl singer, Mindy, the Singing Angel. She had a voice so pure and so sweet and she'd sing the old hymns the way I liked 'em.

There was the Calvary Boys, too. They sang harmony like I remember hearin' the few times Grannie Hoover took me to church as a little girl afore I went away to the School for the Blind.

There's something about sittin' next to a radio in the middle of the night and how that radio takes you away from where you're at to a far way place. Over time, I listened less and less to the radio. It got harder and harder to tune in the radio preachers and more and more stations gave up playin' gospel.

I did listen regular to *The Make Believe Ballroom* show, but when that went off the air and they started playin' all that rock n' roll music, I stopped turning it on at night.

I used to like the radio dramas too. They was perfect for blind folks 'cause they was made for hearing.

Sometime later on when TV came in, I'd be somewhere where there was a TV and try listening to the comedies or soap dramas, but so much was for seeing on the screen. When the Amos 'n' Andy show came to TV, it was all sight gags and pratfalls and such. It took imagination like radio, but there wasn't enough there for me to follow along, being blind and all. I always felt like I was missing most of the show on TV 'cause a' course I couldn't see the gags, so when those people, if they was real people, started laughing, I didn't know what they was laughin' about so I stopped listenin' on TV.

I used to love to listen to *Amos 'Andy, Gene Autry, The Lone Ranger, Arthur Godfrey and his Talent Scouts*, and *The Bob Hope Show*. Oh, and I liked *Jack Benny* and his Negro servant Rochester, and *George Burns and Gracie Allen*. There was so many of those old shows, but they're pretty much all gone now. Don't ask me why, people like me seemed to like 'em and sometimes'd talk about 'em the next day.

The doll stuff started about three years after Ginger and me had been workin' in New York for a couple of years. I don't know how exactly, but I began to miss Anna something terrible. I'd have dreamings about her every night and I could never see her exactly in the dreams, but I always knew it was her I was dreamin'.

We'd be doing this or that together... you know what mothers and daughters do like spic and spanning around the house or stringin' beans or bakin' biscuits... you know, household things. Sometimes, we'd be walkin' in a field and hear a brook in the distance. I like to believe that Anna lives here in New York nearby in a nice apartment and all. As I told earlier, she is not blind and though I don't much see her, she comes over while I'm workin' and tidies up after me. 'Course I'm falsifyin' on all this, but I like to believe she's nearby.

When I was at the School for the Blind, they had dolls in the playroom and I didn't much like dolls then. They didn't seem to be like babies at all. Their faces was rubbery and their arms and legs only moved in one direction. They didn't have real hair but only rubber- shaped hair. I suppose not seeing and all, I depended more on how they felt rather than how they looked, like other girls. So I was never much interested in dolls when I was a girl.

One day a mother and her daughter stopped to listen to me and Ginger singing a show tune. I heard them stop nearby and the mother say to the little girl that she had seen the show we was singin' the song from before she was married when it first opened. After we was done, the mother gave the little girl some coins and told her to put them in my cup. She walked up and dropped the coins into my cup and I thanked her like I always do. I asked her her name and she said, Carrie. Usually, people leave right after giving us some pay, but I sensed she was still there looking at me and then, to my surprise, she asked if I wanted to see her dolly. Her mother corrected her and said the reason we was singin' was cause we was blind and that I couldn't see her dolly, but I could hold her. So being polite and all, I said I'd like to hold her dolly.

Well, I don't know what happened, but the tears began to pour out of my dried-up, old eyes. I cradled that little girl's dolly like you would hold your baby if you was about to lose it. The little girl saw me and asked if I had a dolly when I was a little girl and I just up and said "Yes, and her name was Anna." 'Course I was falsifyin' again. Her mother sounded nervous and said, "Come on Carrie, we've got to go home. It's late." So I held the dolly out to her and she took it and they left.

I asked Lewis if he knew where there was toy store nearby and he told me where and on the way home, I bought a real nice doll. I lied to the young woman that it was for my daughter, when really it was her in a way. I'd never felt a doll that seemed so real. It took all my earnings and then some, but I didn't care.

I sometimes use big words that's taught to blind folks and people think I'm being uppity and using uptown words to show off, but truth be told, they often mean special things to us, like the word "palpate," which means to touch or feel, but it has special meaning to a blind person who is compensating for not seeing.

Well, since I couldn't see my new dolly, I palpated her all over and she felt so real, not like those dolls we had in the Kansas School for the Blind where I learned the word. She didn't smell rubbery like the old dolls we played with. She was so cold when I unwrapped her and took her out of her box... 'cause we'd just gotten home and her little body was all cold, so I held her tight to my chest until she was warm like I was and then she felt real to me, even her hair.

That night in my chair, I just sang a whole 'nother workday of songs and hymns and cradled that little girl 'til I fell asleep. I even sang some of the "tired mother" lullabies I remembered hearing as a young'un. I didn't think they was funny when I was little but, 'course, a colicky newborn howlin' all day and makin' momma crazy while she's trying to be a wife and mother and doin' chores and all, couldn't understand the words of the song. The melody was a soft lullaby that soothed the baby, but the words was angry words so the mother could let off her steam.

My favorite was:

Today is the day we give babies away with a half a pound of tea.
If you know any ladies who want any babies, send them around to me.

Another meaner one, though it makes me laugh when I hear it in my mind was:

What'll we do with the baby? What'll we do with baby-o?
What'll we do with baby? Send him off to his mammy-o.
That's what we do with the baby-o. (chorus)

Every time the baby cries, we stick our fingers in the baby's eyes.

Chorus
Every time he starts to grin, we give the baby a bottle of gin.

Chorus
Put him up in the old tree top; the wind will blow and the cradle will rock.

Chorus
Wrap him up in the table cloth; throw him up in the old hayloft.

Chorus

That big doll made me so happy. Soon, I bought another and another. Ginger thought I'd gone crazy on dolls.

'Course, I never bought one single doll that disadvantaged Ginger's share of our workin' money. There was nights and a few days, though, where I didn't have nothing to eat 'cause I'd bought another new doll.

Finally, when I had a lot of dolls around, I knew I had to have a talkin' to with myself. There's no one in my life to do that but me, so I sat myself down one night and had a talkin'-to.

I thought about some of the men on my floor who I'd hear at night crashin' their drunken way down the corridor to their little rooms and sometimes sleepin' in the dark corridor 'cause they lost their key, and about how they couldn't stop drinkin' themselves to death.

I simply said to myself that I had enough dolls and that I wouldn't buy any more. When I'd come home after workin' all day, though, and have someone to hold and sing to and share my supper with, it'd feel good and I knew then I was mournin' on Anna. It'd "releviate me some," as Ginger likes to say.

Now, y'already know I'm a preacher. Like I told, I wasn't ordained by no high fallutin' ministry official, but when I was attendin' a prayer meeting near where I live, the preacher took me aside and blessed me with the power to minister onto other folks after he heard me testify and sing a few hymns to Jesus. Ginger, 'course, got all huffy 'cause I got chose for somethin'. So bein' a good Christian minister, he anointed her my Deaconess of Music 'cause she had an accordion and all and sang such sweet harmonies. Ginger seemed satisfied with that title, so ever since then, least on Sundays, we've been The Reverend Baybie Hoover and Virginia Brown, the Deaconess of Music.

We started our little church about four years ago 'cause blind folks was comin' by sometimes and listening to our songs. They couldn't give us no money 'cause they didn't have none to give, but they'd sometimes stop when we was breakin' for a rest for a bit and ask us questions and all about where we learned our songs and all.

There was a building on 48th Street here — you know, the apartment house — and we got a little place there and leased it and we got a little church there and I started preaching again. But before we got this church, I went to Brooklyn to Brother Sparrow, a minister that we knew of, and he examined me. I told him, you know, that I'd been called to preach, and he examined me, and you know he asked me Bible questions. He gave me an examination and I passed it. And so one Saturday night, well, you know, we joined his church and on Saturday night I was ordained by this Brother Sparrow.

'Course he's dead now. And this time I was really ordained and licensed. You know, he gave me my big paper. Then we had this little church on 48th but they expected us to do all the repairs and we just didn't have the money enough to swing it and finally we lost our lease.

He's a realtor, this Woody, and he found this other place, this 1248 Gates Avenue out in Brooklyn. It's an old building; the landlord was about to sell it, and we went about converting it into a church. It's chartered now by the State of New York. It's small, but enough for us and our little ministry. Ginger may live over that way. I 'spect sometimes she sleeps in the church when it isn't Sunday. We got our charter and everything, so I'm really a regular ordained, licensed minister and I can marry people or perform at funerals and I have all the powers of any other ordained minister.

Six of our faithful's blind, but Leroy isn't and he helps us clean it up and make it nice. It used to be a shop of some kind, but got abandoned. The whole building is empty, he says, and maybe the block 'cause we never hear folks 'round there much. Leroy found us some folding chairs and some fixed ones too and there's a little table where we share our food afterwards and nicest of all, Leroy made me a little lectern where I do my preachin' and Ginger leads us all in song. After cleanin' it up some, Leroy put a padlock on the door and kept a key in case we lost ours, but I keep mine pinned here on my sleeve so I never will lose it and Ginger has one she pins somewhere too.

Oh, it's nothin' fancy like them big-city churches with organs and pews and all, but Ginger has her accordion and we make do. Members of the congregation usually bring some day-old pastries for us to share during sharing time and Milly brings in nice creamy coffee in a big old thermos. I can smell that coffee now. She uses real cream too, not just milk like they do in the corner stores. Riley keeps us in sugar, paper cups, and little wooden stirrers 'cause he works in a deli.

I begin the service with a prayer and invitation to Jesus to join us in our church and to abide with us during our praying and singing time. I then preach a sermon I've thought in my mind the night before at home after prayin' for the Lord's guidance. It'd usually be inspired by a story I'd heard on how Jesus helped someone cope with their tribulations or on how we musn't visit them on others.

After my sermon and a few hymns, we arrange the chairs in a circle for sharing time so nobody's higher up than anyone else and we'se all together. I lead us in a short prayer to ask God to hear our troubles and to help us find our way. Then Virginia leads us in a hymn and then we have sharin' time. Folks like that the best.

We go 'round in a circle, starting in a different place each time. Each person takes as long as they need to share their troubles and trials and the congregation listens and offers up prayers together to relieve that person. There's a rule during sharin' time that there's no interruptin', even to ask questions. In that way, the person gets all their story told and their pain out in the circle before we offer up help and prayers and sympathizings. Sometimes, if Ginger, is inspired by a certain hymn, she'll suggest we sing that hymn together for alleviations.

Now I'm one of those girls that cries at everything sad I hear and I have to try and maintain a preacher face, but ever' so often when I hear one of our faithful testifyin' about what this world has visited on them, I just break down and cry like a baby.

From how I'm describin', you might think it's all sadness and worries, but sometimes, it's also about good things in their lives, something wonderful that happened... like the time Lucy was getting sicker and sicker on her diabetes and couldn't get no help from any of the agencies.

Like me, Lucy lives alone in an SRO but down on the Lower East Side where the neighborhoods aren't so good. Now Lucy makes me look like a skinny-minny; she's a big girl and has lots a trouble moving around and climbin' stairs and such. She was gettin' to the point where she never left her room and was havin' troubles with her hygiene and such.

There came a knock on her door and a nice-looking girl asked to come in. Lucy told how she could hardly get out of her bed to let the girl in — the girl was in her early twenties so I should say she was a woman — turned out to be a daughter Lucy had lost track of during her drinking time. She'd grown into a fine young woman and had a job at an agency that took care of homeless folks so she had wherewithals to help her mother.

When Lucy told us that story, I began to sob like I do, way down in my chest and then just bawled my heart out. 'Course, I was thinkin' on my Anna and how I've always wanted her to come to me that way.

Anyway, I finally gathered myself and said I was sorry for interruptin' and listened on how Lucy's daughter got her mother into the clinic and got her some medicine to help with her diabetes. She also got her into a food kitchen where they help women with malnutrition and overweight and all and soon Lucy was looking and feeling better and better.

The way she told it had us all laughin' and cryin', 'specially when she told on being introduced to all those healthy foods she'd had as a little girl, like grits and greens and beets and peas and catfish and such. They got her eating all these foods like she'd never heard tell of them.

Why, didn't we laugh when she told that part about how she'd just pretend to the nurse it was all new to her, sayin', "Oh, isn't that good and oh, isn't this delicious." Course, she was doin' it to make them feel good about their service to her and all. She said it was like being home again, sprinkling vinegar on the collard greens and all.

Like me sometimes, and lots of folks that have to live on very little or can't get enough work to buy good food, she'd gotten into eating day-olds and other people's leftovers. She even told on going into great big restaurants where they didn't guard the door and where it would take 'em awhile to clean up, and how she'd eat the rest of the food off'n other people's plates, even picking butts out of French fries and gravy and eating what's left. Thankfully me and Ginger never had to resort to that, but I can tell you, there was times when we thought on it.

Anyway, here I go again, talking 'bout me and Ginger when my story was about Lucy.

Lucy moved her into her daughter's apartment in Queens where she had a nice sunny bedroom and lots of good food and they became acquainted again, mother and daughter. Turns out when Lucy's daughter came to the Lord herself, she lost her recriminations against her mother that she had when she was a little girl, and told how a kindly preacher had said to her that she needed to find her mother and tell her that she had forgiven her and be a solace to her in her old age.

She followed her preacher's advice and the two live together and have each other for company. Lucy seems much better and though she's still a big woman, she has better health and walks to the store, does shoppin' and makes healthy meals for them while her daughter works. It still tears me up when I think on it.

Some weeks ago, we lost Leonard and no one knows where he went. Leonard did begging with his old dog over near East 57th Street in a fancy-pants neighborhood and he always use to tell how nobody'd give to a nigger, but they'd feel kindly to his old dog and drop a few coins in his hat.

Awhile back, he told us how his dog Ben got sick and how he had to spend his earnings puttin' him down. I never seen a man cry as much as Leonard did tellin' about Benjy and how he got hip pains and couldn't walk right, but he'd always try to follow Leonard wherever he went.

Soon after he told us that story, he stopped comin' to service and we all prayed extra hard for him, but none of us has heard from him since. I know the Lord will take care of him, but he sure did miss that old dog of his.

Why I could tell you stories about our sharin' time into next year, but I 'spect you want to hear more than other people's sadnesses.

When David came to my room, I could sense on how he was surprised by all the dolls, 'cause he asked about 'em. I jess told him they was my little girls and I cared for 'em. He understood then. I liked that about David. He seemed to understand about me and Ginger and we didn't have to explain every little thing to him.

That was the night he asked me about makin' a record. That was exciting to me 'cause a' course I'd heard records as a blind person and learning music and such. Lewis had told me about his collection of race records he had and how much he liked jazz singin' and blues music and all. But most of the music I'd heard on records was at the School for the Blind where we sometimes listened to records and cylinders of words and music. I know now a' course that most of the music I heard on radio was from records, when for a long time, I thought they was people playing it all in the radio studio.

'Course most of the music Ginger and I learned was on the radio, either the old gospel preachin' radio or the ballroom radio shows. We liked both. Sometimes we'd also listen to hillbilly radio when it started, The Carter Family singers and all, but we'd get tired of all that twangin' stuff and men singin' high tenor and the like so it was mostly radio gospel and ballroom, like I said.

I don't know what I liked so about David, but he never asked me for nothin' and always seemed like he was respectin' us. He understood that Ginger and me worked for a living and seemed like he had, too, since he understood how hard our work could be and it meant somethin' to him that Ginger and I could sing a hundred songs without ever repeatin'.

He didn't seem stranged when I told him about Anna like she was with me. He'd ask when I saw her and such, and even though he knew I was falsifyin' he didn't seem to care. He asked my permission to make recordings of our story-telling and explained to me how it was done. He let me touch the little recorder he had with him. At first, I thought he said it was a "Negro" and I got all confused, and then he pronounced it like it was supposed to be and I understood that it was a make of recorder... a "Nagra." He explained to me how the sounds went through a microphone and got lodged on a ribbon of tape. It amazed me 'cause I'd only heard tell about records and didn't understand how the music got on them.

Anyway, he'd come by my room on nights we agreed and record. He'd always bring me somethin' nice to eat and first we'd share some supper. He'd sit on my cot and I'd sit in my favorite chair. David didn't do much talkin'. He'd ask me some questions and, 'course, me bein' me, it'd just start pourin' out. I asked him if he was gonna record Ginger as well and he said he'd like to if she'd let him, but like I said, Ginger isn't much of a talker and some of what she says ain't fit for puttin' on a record 'cause she ain't always nice in choosin' her words. I wouldn't want no one making a record of me sayin' nasty things on it.

David'd always leave at eleven, bein' mindful of my workday. He'd always say, "Well, that's it for tonight. You have a busy day ahead."

I don't know what else he did for work, but he'd always be talkin' like he was thinking of me and I appreciated him for that. Not many folks I met is like that. It was nice havin' a visitor too, 'specially one you could trust bein' with. I'd miss David on nights he wasn't there; 'course I had Anna.

David had earned my trust, but Virginia wasn't the trustin' type and he had quite a time winnin' Ginger over. Like I said earlier, somethin' must have happened to her that made her so wary of everybody. I think I was the only person she trusted, but not a' course enough to tell me where she lived. Sometimes, people get secretive when they'se ashamed, but Ginger ain't ever done anythin' bad that I heard tell from her. I suspect it's bads that been done to her what made her the way she is.

Anyway, David still had to earn her trust. She didn't come out and say anythin' direct, 'cause she don't. She just kept her distance. When he was on the street with us and we'se takin' a rest, she'd answer questions she wanted and simply ignore the rest.

It seemed, though, like David had an understanding of her ways 'cause he never pushed her on what she didn't want to say, but would encourage on what she did want to talk on and Ginger could be a real show-off, you know when she felt like it. If David asked her something she knew about, she'd start yappin' away like a preacher on whatever he asked and I think, this way, David gradually earned Ginger's trust, at least on maybe making a record of us singing together.

Sometimes street people would steal our money, small as it was. We didn't earn enough money in a day to be much worth their stealin', but I guess they was too dumb or too chicken to rob and steal for real, like banks and stores where there was real money to be had, so they'd just prey on poor folks like themselves. It didn't happen that often 'cause we worked in a place where there was always lots of people comin' and goin' all the time and we'd stay as close to Bloomingdale's as Lewis would let us. Sides' I always had the feeling that Lewis was keepin' an eye out on us as part of his job greetin' and helping rich people goin' in and out of his store and carryin' parcels and helpin' 'em get taxis and such.

Ginger, like I told, couldn't be bothered holding her cup if she wasn't playin' her 'ccordion. She'd pin her cup to her chest and, like I said, most people still don't like approachin' a blind person 'cause of what Ginger said about sex diseases blindin' folks and all. I'd always hold my cup out and get most of the giving.

One day — it was bright and sunny and there was lots of people on the street — a man ran up and grabbed my cup out of my hand. I usually empty money out so the cup isn't so heavy, and, also, you want people to think that other folks's giving you money, but not so much that you don't need it. He couldn't have gotten away with more than a few dollars, but he took it anyway. I hated loosing my cup more 'cause each time I'd have to buy a new one. It was easy enough finding an ol' coffee cup or the like, but they're heavy and I need a tin measuring cup and they're harder to find and I'd usually have to buy a new one at the hardware.

Anyway, David came by later that day to ask if it was okay to come by that night after we finished working and record us talking about how we came to New York and where we learned our songs and all. I said sure, and I told him about the man running up and stealing my cup. I asked Ginger to come along and see what it was like. She'd been to my place many times like I told when we was first in New York, even though I'd never been to hers, if she had one. I didn't even know.

We agreed that we'd get up to my place around 5:30. Ginger'd just come home with me. When we packed up and left around 4:30, 'cause it was chilling down, I checked the cup and there was a couple of bills in there so I asked Lewis to sort 'em out like he did and when I got them back I was surprised he'd folded up a twenty. I know David put it in there 'cause I heard a man approach when he was there on the sidewalk and he wasn't talkin'. I can't know for sure, but I'd bet a dime to a dollar that David put that twenty in there when he heard about the man stealing my cup. He's that way, I came to know.

When he showed up at my room, he brought me a nice new tin cup and he got some lasagna for the three of us to share. 'Course I could smell it the minute I got up to let him in. It was nice, like havin' a family and all. Course, silly me, I didn't have no proper table settin' stuff, in fact I didn't have no table, 'cause I always ate alone, so we all just sat around and shared the tinfoil lasagna plate, passin' it around and sharin' my fork. It almost tears me up to think on it. I could tell that Ginger, too, was on her best behavior, not makin' her usual judgments and grousings. It was a wonderful evening and I don't think I'll ever forget it or have another one like it, though we did after we made the recordin', but I'll tell more on that later.

So that night David explained to us about how we'd make a record of our songs. 'Course, silly me, I thought we was makin' a 78 with one song on one side and another on the other side. I'd never heard tell of a 33 or what he kep' callin' an album record. He explained that he could put ten or fifteen songs on one record. 'Course it was bigger'n a 78, but only two inches, he said, and it had a nice picture cover and all. He promised to bring me one to hold so I could get a better idea of it. 'Course I had no way to play it 'cause I didn't have a gramophone.

I missed hearin' music other than what me and Ginger made together, but like I told, the radio just didn't have any music that we liked so I never turned it on.

Sometimes, on my way home, I'd go by another group of street singers, but they was singin' popular music like the Ames Brothers and some was singing a kind of music I never heard with a lot of nonsense words like "shebop" and "doowah" and the like it. I sort of liked it, though some of it sounded like starvin' cat music to me.

That night after supper, David explained the plan to Ginger and me on how we'd make the record. He lived up north in a town called Vermont. He'd put us on a bus at the same station we came into and then he'd fly up on an airplane and meet us on the other end. Neither Virginia or I was goin' anywhere in no airplane, but we had traveled a lot together by bus. We didn't want to miss the holiday season when we made most of our money, so we agreed that we would go up to David's right after Christmas and come home right after New Year's 'cause nothin' happened between those two days and no one was on the street again until the day after New Year's.

The only change in plan was that David had a trusty friend who lived down here who would take us to the bus and help us get on and get comfortable and all so he wouldn't have to fly down again. He offered to introduce us to his friend, who was a doctor, but I'd come to trust David and what he recommended. So if he trusted his friend, I could too. 'Course I's never sure with Ginger whether she was lip servin' or trustin' him. I'm not sure Ginger could ever trust anyone, even me sometimes.

The holidays was good for Ginger and me; we done better'n we usually do. Each day, we'd make sometimes thirty or forty dollars. On Christmas Eve when we usually make our most, we made about eighty dollars. I never heard so many paper bills goin' into my cup. Even Virginia's cup had money in it, which, like I told, was rare.

We met Dr. John at the bus station like we was supposed. He seemed very nice and talked like he was from England or someplace where they spoke English, 'cause he spoke really well, but had a different accent. Ginger asked him where he was from, right out, like she'll do and he said Australia, which we'd heard of. He told us it was as far away as you could ever be from where we lived. He seemed to know our music as well and told us how much he liked our singing and all. If I recall, it was him that got David acquainted with our singing.

Anyways, he was real good to us. We didn't have much to carry. Ginger had her accordion and I had a small shopping bag with some personals and my cup. I didn't understand why Dr. John said to be sure and bring our cups 'cause we wasn't gonna do no public workin' in Vermont. From David's telling, it sounded a lot like Kansas with very few cities where anyone would gather to hear us sing. Dr. John explained that they would be recordin' the sound of our cup shakin' just like on the street. Now, like I told, Ginger doesn't use her cup, but I brought it anyway just in case. David and Dr. John had been so nice, we wanted to be sure and do right by their kindnesses.

Dr. John found us the right bus in that giant cathedral of comings and goings. He helped us on and then gave me an envelope with some money and a small bag with some sandwiches and juices for us to drink on the trip. He also took time to explain to the driver that we was blind and asked him to keep and eye on us during the long trip to Vermont, 'specially since it was our first trip since comin' to New York way back when.

Ginger, being Ginger, kept asking him her worries like whether he was sure that David would be there to meet us on the other end, if there was a toilet on the bus, what kind of sandwich he got for her, where her accordion was again after he told her for the how manyth time it was on the luggage rack up above. Dr. John was patient with her like David and just answered her silly questions again and again.

Soon we was underway. Now like I told, my way of seein' is with my hearing. 'Course, ya can't hear nothin' on a bus except other folks chit-chattin' and the roar of the big motor. Oh, what I would a given to see the countryside outside a' that cold window. Bein' Christmas and all and since we was headed north, I knew there'd be snow on the ground. David said there'd be tall mountains and lots of lakes and rivers, but I had to imagine it all as best I could. I was wishin' Anna could come with me on this trip, so she could be describing all the beauty rollin' by that cold window.

Ginger wanted to sit in the aisle so's she could go to the bathroom when she needed. I always find it's easier to just give in to Ginger when she wants something, otherwise there's an eternity of fussin' and if she doesn't get what she wants, she pouts for the longest time like a spoiled little girl. I don't mind givin' in to her wants now and then though, 'cause I know one thing for sure, ain't never been no spoilin' in her life.

Sittin' close on her for that amount of time, I did begin to worry again about her hygiene and Dr. John did ask her some questions about if she had access to facilities where she lived, but like any questions she doesn't like or know the answer to, she just says nothing. See when Ginger and I're together, we're outdoors most of the time, so I don't smell her much, but in that cramped up bus seat like we was, I came to know that she needed some help with her hygiene and all. 'Course I didn't say anything on the bus, 'cause I didn't want a fuss with all those people, but I didn't want to be in the recording and have everyone worryin' on Ginger and her smelling bad.

Other than my worryin' on Ginger not being clean and all, the bus trip was pretty regular and put us both in a mind of our many trips on the way. When we wasn't snoozin' we recalled those long trips across from Kansas to New York and all the places we stopped and sang to add to our savings and have a hot meal. 'Course it was warm enough and we could sleep outside if we had to. We was younger then and had to worry about being bothered by men with bad thoughts about young women.

The whole trip was only eight hours and we both got a good rest. When the bus driver told we was coming into Burlington, Vermont, we gathered our belongings and got ready to get off, but it was still a few minutes before the bus stopped and made that loud whoosh that busses make when they are finally done movin'.

We waited until all the other passenger was off and then Ginger got off and made room for me to get my bag and hand her down her accordion. We then walked to the front of the bus hangin' on to the seat backs until the driver asked us if he could help and he took our things and helped us down the steep steps onto the platform.

The first voice I heard over the public address announcements echoing in the background was David's. He welcomed us and asked about the trip. Ginger, her usual self, groused about a few things, but all and all agreed that it was pretty easy. We thanked David as well for the kindnesses of Dr. John and told him that he had been very nice to us.

I guess the bus station in Burlington was a lot smaller than the one in New York 'cause first of all there was no echo. It sounded like we was in a small place with soft walls, and second the car was only a short walk from where we got off the bus. David left the car running so it was warm when we loaded in and Ginger kept askin' about her accordion and David assured her that he had it in the car. I think it was the new surroundings that made Ginger nervous and questionin' everything like she always does when she's worryin'.

David seemed to know about bein' blind and all, 'cause all the way to where we was going, he described where we was goin' and what the countryside looked like. He said there was a blanket of snow covering everything. He and Dr. John both had a way of talkin' that painted pictures for Ginger and me about what they was seein'.

Most folks'll just say "Oh, there's a hitchhiker," which doesn't tell a blind person anything, while David or Dr. John would know to say, "Oh, there's a young man with long hair and a backpack and he's thumbin' a ride in the other direction."

They both seemed to have a sensitiveness about what it means to be a blind person and how they could bridge the blind person over to having a better idea of what they was sayin' by imaging inside themselves what it means to be blind. Now, I didn't say that very well, but you know what I mean. It's like trying to imagine how another person feels rather than only acting on what you, yourself, feel. Jesus talks about this in the Bible, course in a much better way than I just did.

I try to preach on this sometime to our little congregation, but it's hard to talk about unless you're blind yourself. The people in our little church are mostly all blind like Ginger and me, so they understand my preachin' and singing and say "Amen, sister" to let me know they understand my meaning.

David didn't know about our little church, so that evening when we'd settled in to our motel room near the recording studio, David brought his little recorder and asked us to tell on how our little church started and where it was. But I'm getting' ahead of myself again.

We didn't know where we would be sleeping, which always makes us uneasy, 'cause so many times, we've had to sleep in places where we didn't feel safe from predacious men. And when you don't feel safe where you are, it's hard to sleep. You keep waking up at every noise and have to decipher what kind of noise it is, where it's coming from and if it's a threatening noise or just some noise in the night like is normal.

Now, we ain't no pin-up girls anymore, but some men don't even care when the devil's got a hold on their carnal instincts.

David said there was no private sleeping quarters at the recording studios so he got us a cozy little room at a motel close by where he knew the owner. He described it to us so it made it sound wonderful, and when we got there it was. We'd never stayed in a hotel or motel before so David toured us around the room. There was two beds and a private bathroom with nice smelling soap and all. He showed us how we could lock and unlock the door so's we could sleep soundly and not worry about anyone coming in while we was asleep. It was real nice. The sheet's was clean and ironed. There was a big comfy chair. There was a TV and all, but we don't listen to TV cause it's too hard to turn on and all.

We went straight there 'cause we'd had our last sandwiches on the bus and we was so excited about bein' in our room, we couldn't even think on eatin'. I sat in the big chair just like I do at home and Ginger put her feet up on the bed like she likes settin' up there, leanin' on a pile a pillows like the Queen of Sheba. If that girl could smile, I bet she was then. We both suffer from our feet swellin' so I know she liked bein' there. Course, she'd never let on.

I asked Ginger if she wanted tell on some sharin' she remembered.

But Ginger was tired and didn't have nothin' to say. I think we was all tired. On the bus, I couldn't get comfortable in that little seat for more than a few minutes and kept shiftin' which'd wake up Ginger, and she kept having to get up and go to the bathroom. Lucky they had one on that bus. I guess they do now on all the long bus trips. Good thing, too.

I think what struck us more than any other thing on being in Vermont, was the silence. Now, to a blind person, even silence has a low rumble to it. I don't know how to describe it. I heard a blind preacher call it "the firmament sound that only blind folks can hear" but that didn't tell me anything. It was a like a very quiet low bass note on Ginger's accordion playing all the time, real quiet in the background. We hadn't heard that sound ever since we came to New York where we only heard the sound of a subway roaring by underneath us.

It was deathly quiet and it took us time to get used to it. It reminded me of my time on the prairie where you could hear an owl hoot, or a rabbit scream or the distant whistle of a freight train passing a grade crossing. Even though our motel was near the road, I only heard a truck roll by once or twice in the night. I slept "the sleep of the dead" as old Buzz used to say.

Ginger and me slept like babies in between our nice clean sheets and David made sure that the room was warm enough for us 'cause it sure was cold outside.

The next morning, David came to fetch us and we was ready. Ginger always gets up early; fact I'm never sure how much she sleeps.

We was surprised to hear that the recording studio was an old cow barn that had been all made nice inside. Course we had no idea what a studio would even look like. The minute we stepped inside, I knew that the ceilings was high like a church and I said something like "oh, my" like I might have seen it, but I just wanted the sound so I could measure how big the space was by my hearing.

David was good, and he described everything. Like I said, he had a sensitiveness about us being blind and all. He had asked another singer he recorded to come over and be with us in case we had any questions about singing and recording. Her name was Sara Cleveland and she sang country songs like we did but not so much about the Lord and saving souls as about telling stories. We was very happy to meet another woman our age who had grown up singing and all.

She was the first to know the problem with Ginger and didn't think twice about asking her. I learned a lot from Sara that way. After she and Virginia shared some talk about their past and all, Sara said to Ginger, You smell like you ain't had a bath in a year. Even before Ginger could get angry or work up a fuss, she just answered, that it'd been longer than that 'cause there weren't no facilities where she stayed most of the time. She said she wouldn't use a bathtub 'cause she was always afeared she couldn't get outta one once she got in.

Well, let me tell you, Sara took the matter right in hand and told Virginia that she was going to have her first bath and that she would give it to her and that Virginia would enjoy it. There wasn't even time for Ginger to work up some reason not to. Sara led her into the bathroom in that studio and began helping her take her clothes off. Ginger even seemed to like being mothered like that and didn't put up her usual fuss.

I guess from listening on Sara, it was pretty bad though. She had to ask for scissors 'cause Ginger's hair had grown through a head cap she wore and Sara had to cut it off outside the hat before she could remove it and then she found poor Ginger had head lice. I'm glad I didn't know 'cause I'm terrible afraid of lice from when I was a little girl and Mrs. Desmets used to rub my hair with kerosene to kill lice even when I didn't have any.

Sara handed Ginger's clothes out to David and told him to burn them outside. Sara told later that Ginger was all covered with rashes and she had to wash her real careful so as not to wash off skin in certain parts. Her toenails had grown around the ends of her toes and had to be cut real careful so as not to have her get an infection in her feet. It was worse than I'd ever imagined. Couple times, we heard Sara speak in a forceful but motherly voice to Virginia to get her to move around in the tub so Sara could clean her up. Sara was strict, but kindly to Ginger. I was glad Ginger was getting clean and all, but I felt sorry for her in a strange place, but later I learned she was grateful to Sara.

When she was done — it must have been an hour — Sara asked David to come in and help lift Ginger out of the tub. He went in and helped Sara and then fetched a bed sheet while Sara dried Ginger all over and then wrapped her up in the bed sheet. Lucky it was warm in that studio!

I stayed with Ginger and we sat on the couch and practiced our singing while David and Sara went into town to get some clothes for Ginger. Sara must've guessed Ginger's size, 'cause when they came back, they had some nice things for her, from underthings up to a nice blue and white cotton dress.

I wish I could a seen her all dressed up like a queen. She seemed pretty pleased with herself 'cause Sara kept sayin', "There, there, now don't you just look nice and pretty and all in your new cotton shift."

I know when Ginger's smilin''cause she's too busy smilin' and bein' happy to make a fuss.

I was shamin' myself 'cause I was wishin' how someone would give me a bath and wash my back and all and put me in some nice new clothes, but then I've always been good about my personal hygiene. I buy new underwear when I need to and keep myself clean. There's no bathroom in my room, like I said, but the one down the hall smells clean in the morning and I use it right after they clean it early morning before the men get back at night and make a mess again. I wish they had a bathroom just for ladies like they do in restaurants and hotels. Men and women's different, and you get a man liquored up and he'll pee just about anywhere.

So after they got Ginger all gussied up and sittin' on the couch like queenie and all, Sara suggested we sing together. I never heard Ginger so agreein' on everything. We sat down and sang some songs Sara knew and we taught her a few she'd never heard.

Sara had a high lonesome sound to her singing. Her voice quavered like an elderly lady might when she sang but her pitch was perfect, even though her hearing wasn't. She sang us a beautiful, sad song called, "In the Pines."

The longest train I ever saw
Went down that Georgia line
The engine passed at six o'clock
And the cab passed by at nine.

Chorus:
In the pines, in the pines
Where the sun never shines
And we shiver when the cold wind blows;
Whooee-whoo-hoo; whoo-hoo-hoo
Whooee-whoo-whoo-hoo-hoo

I asked my captain for the time of day
He said he throwed his watch away
A long steel rail and a short cross tie
I'm on my way back home.

Chorus

Little girl, little girl, what have I done
That makes you treat me so?
You caused me to weep, you caused me to mourn
You caused me to leave my home.

Chorus

I shoulda told earlier that Sara was sighted and probably twenty years older than we was. She really could've been our mother. Anyway, David having her there and all made it twice as easy for us to get comfortable and even though David helped Sara with Ginger, it wouldn't have been right for him to give her a bath the way Sara did.

We sang together, swappin' songs and stories until we had some supper, though David didn't do any recording, sayin' that we would start recording tomorrow. I asked if Sara could stay and she said she could, she'd like to hear us sing some more of our songs.

After we had supper and said our good nights, David drove us back to where we was staying. Sara stayed in the room next door 'cause she had come over from upstate New York, and Ginger and I talked into the night. I never heard Ginger talk so much or be so happy. It's as if just cleaning her up washed away all that suspicion and anger she'd built up in her. Then, o' course, all that silence eased us both a bit and made us pay more attention to what we was doing than trying to decipher the din.

'Course I knew it wouldn't last and worried if it would be more years afore she bathed again. I worry still that she has no access to bathing facilities, much less the other kind.

David picked us up the next day and took us to breakfast at a little diner nearby where we had eggs and toast and bacon. It was the kind of breakfast you can only get in a diner, real good with hot coffee and milk and all. Then we piled back into David's warm car and drove back to the studio. I wish I could have seen that studio. Sara said it looked just like the cow barn it was on the outside. The only way she said you could tell it was people in there, instead of cows was a few big picture windows that looked out into the fields. I always thought phonograph records was made in radio stations, but what did I know on that?

Like I said, David was real good about explainin' everything he did, though I'm not sure Ginger and me understood half of what he was tellin' us. Sometimes Sara, who had made a record with David as well, would put what he was sayin' in words we could better understand 'cause she'd been through the recordin' and all herself.

Since we only recorded one song at a time and could redo it as many times as we wanted. I felt better singing standing up. Ginger did too. When you sit down and you're a big woman like Ginger and me, it pushes on your stomach and you don't have as much to give to the singing as you should. 'Course singin' all day outdoors like we do at home, I have to sit down and so does Ginger to keep from getting' too tuckered out.

While we was singin' we used our tin cups that we brought to show people listening to our songs on record that we was workin' while we was singin'. I'd shake mine if Ginger was playin' the accordion and we'd both shake ours in rhythm with the music if she wasn't, kinda like a tambourine.

On the day we recorded Dr. John showed up and it was like we was a family, Ginger, me, Sara, David, and Dr. John and his friend Priscilla.

We spent all day recording but David always asked us if we was tired and wanted to take a break. Ginger was so full a piss and vinegar from her being clean and all, she kept saying "Let's do more, let's do more." I think she thought she was becoming a star or something. It was nice to see her feelin' so good after so many years of feeling bad about herself.

We recorded about ten songs then stopped and had supper. We was all tired and so retired early, but sweet Sara asked that since I was a minister and all if we could have a service in the barn before we started recording on Sunday. I was flattered that she thought on that and I know Ginger was 'cause she started sayin' her "Oh, yes, oh, yes, let's."

So Sunday morning after we had our little breakfast at the diner, we all gathered up at the studio barn and David made me a preachin' spot with a music stand. He asked if he could record our service and we all said yes. 'Course we all forgot he was recording when it came to sharin' time, so we all didn't worry 'bout what we shared.

After I led us in a prayer and thanked the Lord for our little family and asked him to watch after my small flock in New York, I gave a gratitude sermon for us all being together and for the chance to sing and make a record together.

Then Virginia led us in three hymns that she chose and I asked Sara if she would like to lead us in a song or two. She picked two songs, "Let Us Gather by the River" and "What a Friend We Have in Jesus." Then Ginger and I sat down on the couches with the others and we had our sharin' time.

Ginger and me shared that we had a lot to be grateful for, and I again asked for blessings on Anna and asked the Lord to watch over her and see that we was united one day again on earth.

Sara shared that her brother-in-law had taken to drink after his retirement and was having a terrible time giving up his bottle and she asked God to help him and to bring him back to sobriety and into the bosom of his children, where he had been for so many years before he took up drink.

I have to say it was somethin' funny listenin' to David and Dr. John and his friend trying to share some pain or happiness in their lives. They just wasn't use to our kind of sharin' that way and being open about tribulations or those things they were grateful for. It didn't come easy to 'em. David just listed his gratitudes and thanked us all for being there and all. Some folks just keep a lot of stuff bottled up in 'em and they don't know that sharin'll relieve their pain.

By Sunday night we was done. David took us to a nice restaurant in a town nearby and we had a good meal together. I had pork chops and Ginger had meatloaf that she likes so much. It was some of the best eatin' I ever had and there was seconds and all and all the bread and butter you could eat up and they'd just bring more. Poor Ginger wanted to pack up the rest of the food and bring it home with her to New York.

Sara was especially kindly and said such nice things about our music and how she would tell people about it 'cause she sometimes sang at folk festivals and people cared about where she got her music and all. She also promised to buy one of our records when they came out. I don't think Ginger and I ever felt so honored as we felt that evening with all the good food and love that people showed to us.

The next day, David said we wouldn't have to take the bus back to New York 'cause Dr. John and his nice friend Priscilla, who was also a famous singer, were driving back and he offered to give us a ride. Sara's daughter drove over from New York State and picked her up, but she lived closer by and said she'd be home in two hours.

After all that good carin' and friendship I can tell you it was hard for Ginger and me to go back to work in the winter cold that following Tuesday, though we was both rested and all. I tried to tell Ginger to keep herself clean like she was in Vermont, but she didn't answer, like she doesn't when she doesn't like what she hears.

Anyway, we went back to work and Lewis asked where we'd been, if we was OK and I told him about our trip to Vermont and our recording and all and I think he thought I was fabricatin', 'cause he just said in his way "Yes, yes, isn't that grand."

Ginger, 'course hearing the doubt in his voice, chimed in and added more what happened while we was away. Lewis was very nice and trustin' 'n' all, but I guess we just didn't look like recording people so he just took in what we said, but I don't 'spect he believed any of it.

I didn't worry none, though 'cause when our record'd come out in the spring, I was gonna give one to Lewis for all his many kindnesses to us over the years and then he would know that what we'd told him about being up in Vermont and makin' a record and all would be gospel truth.

January was hard. There was a little warming in the later part, but then February froze up like a freezer locker and there was days where Virginia and I would only work for a few hours, even though the money was good.

You see, the more miserable the weather, I think, the more kindly people feel towards us for singin' 'em a song and warmin' 'em up a bit and they put more in my cup. It's hard to tell what makes some folks tick, but they seem to be more generous in bad weather, and I can tell you there was plenty of it in January and February. It began to warm up in March and 'course there was no way David could be in touch with us 'cause neither Ginger or me had a telephone.

Funny how everday we'd sing about "The Royal Telephone to Jesus," but neither of us had one. When I was at the School for the Blind, they taught us how to get an operator and tell her what or who we was lookin' for, but the street telephones now you have to put money in and dial 'em yourself, least that's what I'm told, which I can do if I know the number, but I don't really have anyone I need to call.

I think the hard weather began to take its toll on Ginger, 'cause sometimes she'd just go silent and all, not, mind you, in the middle of a song, but when we'd agree on a number or I'd just lead into one as I usually do and she'd be silent, no harmony.

Now there's some songs where I sing lead and Ginger sings harmony and if she don't sing, it's still a song, but there's other songs that is only meant as harmony duets and neither part by itself makes up a whole song. So if Ginger doesn't sing her part, the song sounds terrible and don't mean much 'cause I'm just hung out there singin' one harmony part by my lonesome. Kind a like when only one person shows up to church for the wedding.

I began to worry about Ginger 'cause she seemed poutier than usual and I thought maybe all that warmth and fellowship we'd had in Vermont made a contrast in her about what our real life was like.

Oh, I wish I know'd where that girl lived and how she lived and all 'cause I might a been able to help her make it better, but she was so independent, havin' always to do it her way that she just wouldn't let no one help her.

I kep' on offering to bring her to my agency and see if we couldn't get her an apartment like mine. Least-wise she'd have a room and a place to bathe and all, but ever time I'd mention it to her, she'd just clam up like I was a mother hen scoldin' her. I don't know why she was so independent-minded and all. She must a had some terrible upbringings or bad times in her girlhood, but then again, I did too, and I felt like I knew when to trust people and ask for help and all. 'Course, I also had Anna, even though I didn't see her except in my dream time, and Ginger had no one except me.

Late in March, I think it was, Ginger and me was singin' on the Lexington side 'cause there was more sun and we could feel the heat better and after we finished singin' "Jesus, Won't You Come by Here?", we both heard a familiar voice and it was David. We was both so excited, seemed like Ginger came out of her pout for awhile hearing David's voice. He told us that he brought us some records and that he had some with him and would leave the rest back at my place when we was done singin'.

He asked if we might go out to dinner with him that night to celebrate all our hard work together. I asked if Sara and Dr. John and his friend would be with us, but he said that they were busy and he could only stay one day himself before he had to go back to his work recordin' and all.

David handed both me and Ginger a new record. 'Course, I'd never touched one of them album records and was surprised when it was square, but then realized that was plastic wrapping over the cover of the record. Oh, what we wouldn't have given to see the pictures on the cover.

David took the time to carefully show us how to use a thumbnail to open the record jacket like a paring knife to slice down through the wrapping to get at the cover inside. We was both surprised to see that the album cover opened up like a book and there was an inside as well as a front and back, like a picture book.

Well, didn't Ginger come out of herself all of a sudden and flood David with questions as she touched the cover all over and took out the record. She asked David what all the writin' said about her and David told her to read it herself, whereon she got pouty again and didn't say nothing.

David took the cover from her and reached into the pocket where the record was and took out a sheet of paper and handed it to her. Why as soon as Ginger felt the raised point, she got excited and started reading it right there on the sidewalk.

David had had our story tapes transcribed into Braille so that the folks in our church who could read and other blind folks could read and hear our story for themselves.

Well, I began to feel those big sobs coming up again and tried to get a hold on myself. Last thing I wanted was to break down like a baby and start sobbing on Lex and 59th Street in front of a crowd of onlookers who'd be thinkin' I should be all happy like a recording star or some such.

'Course I was happy, but when some folks who haven't had much practice bein' happy get happy, for some reason they break down cryin' instead of just smiling and bein' happy. That's always been my way, expressin' my joy with tears, like I learned it backwards.

Then I totally forgot about our work until I realized a small crowd had gathered around us to see what all the clamor was about. I could hear them whisperin' about us havin' a record and all and didn't that seem a surprise... that two busker ladies singin' songs on the street would have a record and all!

Ginger was still reading away like she was sitting in a schoolroom somewhere. I could tell from the hubbub there was a crowd jostlin' nearby and that we should use that chance to sing and earn some money.

David put a handful of records in my lap and said we was welcome to sell 'em and that we should sell them for seven dollars each and that we could keep all the money. Well, I couldn't imagine how that came to pass, but I will tell you that by the time our workday ended, we'd sold all them records and I had seventy dollars tucked in my pocket to split with Ginger.

David said he would come by my apartment about seven and we'd go out and have a celebration dinner. He said he brought a hundred records and he'd leave those in my apartment and we could sell 'em as we could. I asked him how much they cost, but he said we could have all the records we wanted forever to sell for free and that was our payment for doing the singing and recording and all. He explained that he'd be trying to sell the records in stores, along with Sara's and Priscilla's and the other records they made, and that's how he'd make his share of the money. He also explained something about us getting more money from the records he sold, but I didn't understand it 'til he explained it later.

I knew Ginger and me wasn't singin' in no hoity-toity supper clubs and didn't expect we'd be on any New York radio shows, so it seemed like a good a deal for Ginger and me, but I didn't know anythin' about the record business. I knew recording stars got rich if they was white and we was white, but only if their songs was on the radio a lot and they sang in the uptown supper clubs and ballrooms. I just felt we could trust David and that our songs could be heard on the radio and by people other than those walking by us on 3rd Avenue or Lex.

Ginger and I was waiting at seven when David came. I noticed when we was indoors and out of the spring breeze blowin' up Lex that Ginger was beginnin' to smell bad again, but I didn't want to say anything to make her upset at our celebrating dinner that night, so I just held my worry inside.

David asked us where we wanted to eat and, for all the years we'd lived here, there was only a few places we knew the names of.

Ginger suggested we eat at the restaurant where Aldo worked, who always had some little leftover treat for me when I came by on my way home. 'Course I didn't know the name of the restaurant but I knew right where it was and it wasn't far so we decided to go have dinner there. I was thinking, too, that it would be a nice way to thank Aldo for all his kindnesses even though I 'spect it wasn't his restaurant.

Anway, it was a grand evening. I guided David and Ginger to the alleyway where I would get my little box of treats from Aldo. Then David led us around to the front door. He said "Tonight, we'll eat in the dining room with the other patrons."

Around front, the restaurant had an awning and all on the sidewalk. I could tell as it had begun to sprinkle a bit and when we got out front we was sheltered from the raindrops. David said the place looked real nice. 'Course, bein' David and polite and all, he woulda said that if we'd taken him to a Blarney Stone with steam tables.

I've never been a retirin' type woman and so, when we was to go in, I asked David if he'd take my and Ginger's arms. He said that he'd be honored, and I slipped my arm in his and Ginger did, too. We walked into the restaurant and was greeted by someone with a nice deep Italian voice. David asked for a table for three.

Why, Ginger and me was so proud. I don't usually get puffed up like that, but it felt so good to go into that restaurant by the front door with a nice young gentleman holding my arm and all. I wished Anna could see us then 'cause she would have understood that all I taught her about manners and respect and all was true and that there was indeed good in the world even when most of the time it felt like there wasn't.

Then Aldo spotted us. I never knew whether he worked in the kitchen or the dining room 'cause I'd only meet him at the kitchen door in the alleyway. He'd always ask me how Ginger and me was farin' and would always say, "You take good care now," hand me the box and then go back to his work. In any case, he came right over and made such a fuss over us, tellin' the people he worked with that I was "Baybie" and suddenly everyone seemed interested in us.

David gave him a copy of our record and I introduced him to David. Aldo said he was honored to meet our producer. I had never thought on David as our "producer" and didn't that sound grand to Ginger and me!

I quickly introduced Ginger again to Aldo 'cause she'd only been with me a few times and if she feels out of the center of things she'll take on a pout. So I made a big fuss on her being the Deaconess of Music and all and playing the accordion on the record. David didn't say much but probably couldn't get a word in sidewise with all the fuss and chatter going on around him. It was like old home week in the restaurant. Aldo seemed so proud to see us comin' in the front door and all.

David asked us to order anything we wanted on the menu and I ordered my old favorite, lasagna.

Now, you put Ginger in the spotlight like she was that night and she begins to act like Miss Queenie and all, but we was in no hurry and the waiter patiently explained what all the things listed on the menu were for her benefit.

After hearing the whole list of what the Italian-sounding names were in food she recognized, 'course she ordered lasagna too.

David ordered veal and a salad. I'd heard of it but had never eaten it. Ginger asked on it 'cause she thought it must be some kind of animal she'd never heard of until the waiter explained that it was meat from a newborn calf that had been fed milk.

When the waiter came, our table just filled up with food. The waiter was kindly and told us each plate he put down so we would know which was what and whose was whose. I smelled garlic bread and thought, "Uh-oh. Watch out down below." I love garlic butter bread even though it gives me a sour stomach and that would always be the first thing I ate when I got settled in my big chair at home.

Well, didn't we have a feed! When it came time for dessert, nobody had any stomach room left, but Ginger wanted to know what everything was on the desserts list so the waiter explained it all even though we'd told him we couldn't eat any more.

When it came time to leave, they gave us each a little gift-like box and said they was a dessert called "tiramisu" for us to have later when we got our hunger back. Aldo said they was "on the house" which meant they was free. The waiters was all men and boys and they all came over and made a fuss and congratulated us on our record and all. We left then and David again took our arms and we sashayed right out the front door. People in that restaurant must thought, "Who is them old street ladies, all fussed over and all?"

When we got outside in the cold again, I felt my chest tightnin' up again the way it does when I'm about to tear up. But I didn't sob. I just held tighter on David's arm.

He hailed us a taxi and was going to get one for Virginia, but she told him she didn't trust cab drivers and that she'd take the subway home. It made me wonder on where "home" was for that girl, but she was so private and secretive and all, I just knew I'd never know.

So we walked her to the subway stop for the downtown Broadway line and David walked her down the stair and bought her some tokens and said good night. I know he was worried about her too, but there's some things you just know you can't fix and you have to let 'em be.

We took a cab back to my place. I don't usually take cabs 'cept when it's freezing and the sidewalks are all obstructed with snow and I can't know where I'm goin'. I could use up to half a day's earnings on a taxi and, 'course the driver knows you're blind and can't see the meter, so what he tells you the fare is is what it is. But it felt nice to sit in that big back seat and ride right to my front door at the Markwell.

It was Friday night and Eddy was still cuttin' people's hair in his barber shop so David went in and I introduced 'em 'n' all and they worked out an arrangement for David to send us records to Eddy's shop when we ran out.

'Course, then I get all selfish and thinkin' on if we sell seven records every day — course I knew we wouldn't — we'd need more records every two weeks and then I began thinkin' on how much money that was and what I'd buy and all.

"Silly me," I said. Right then and there I decided that we'd put together a little savings to fix up our church some and help the faithful who come to our church in need with their trials instead of thinkin' on just ourselves.

David and I had a little celebration. He just said he couldn't eat any more so I had my dessert and left his on the shelf to have the next day. I'd never had that tiramisu and it was like food for a queen. I loved the taste of the wet custard and the dry little lady fingers all chocolated. It was one of the best tastes I ever did have.

David said goodnight and told me he'd check in with us tomorrow in case we had any questions or needed any other help. He put his arms around me and gave me a big hug and a little peck on the cheek.

Now, after all that happened to Ginger and me, I'd never been comfortable even being near no man before, but I just felt like cryin' again when David hugged me. It was the kind of hug I would give my Anna and there wouldn't be nothin' threatenin' in holdin' close like that, just tellin on how you

159

loved somebody and respected who they was, and knew their wishes and all and it was okay. No man's ever hugged me that way and I 'spect none ever will again.

The next day was cold but sunshiny and there wasn't no wind to make the cold colder. Ginger came late again and I asked her if everything was okay. She didn't answer like she doesn't when she don't feel like it, so I didn't say nothing more. It's just that it's hard if you're partners and you made your life around singin' together and one or the other doesn't show up or comes late. I can sing about thirty songs by myself and can make a day of it if I have to, but I think it's the harmony that people like listening to and, unless God sends me another voice and I learn to play the accordion and shake the cup at the same time, I can't for the life of me sing lead and harmony alone.

Listen to me again, sounding like a silly girl. You'd think I drank liquor last night. I could smell it in the restaurant, but the devil's never tempted me with alcohol 'cause I know what it can do to people and I often smell it on their breath if they're nearby when I'm singin'.

Some people have a life-of-drink smell that smells more like rubbin' alcohol and just seems to come out of their skin and clothes 'cause they drink all the time. Other folks smell like what they just drank, whiskey or beer or wine, and I've learned to smell the difference.

David stopped by late morning and we chatted for a bit. I thanked him for our celebration dinner and worried that Ginger would just go into a pout for some reason, but she didn't and she was gracious on it, too. David gave us both another hug and I wondered what the folks listening to us must of thought with this young man coming up and giving us both a big hug and talking regular to us like we was somebody or like we was his kin. I wish I coulda seen the look on their faces, but I sometimes don't miss seeing 'cause I can just image what I want and I see in mind all them looking surprised like and tut-tuttin', "How come that handsome young man is givin' them two old buskers a hug like that and talking to them like they was recording stars and all?"

Anyway, we said our goodbyes and I hated to see David go, but knew he would stay in touch with us. I promised him I would send him a letter when we had only twenty records left and he'd then send another hundred to Eddy's barber shop next to where I lived 'cause of David having spoken to Eddy and all.

Oh, how all this goodness made me think on my Anna.

The warm weather made work easier, but Ginger seemed to be getting more erratic in her tardiness and sometime I'd start a harmony song and she'd just not sing along or play her accordion and I'd be hung out there singin' one side of a harmony song by myself and then she'd chime in on the next song like nothing happened. She was coughin' a lot and I began to wonder if she had health problems. Like me, she was a big woman and sometimes had problems with her digestions and her breathin' heavy and all.

I finally decided to have a reckonin' with her and ask her to let me help her with her lodgin's or her ailments or tribulations or whatever was troublin' her. I explained that our sojourn and our church were missioned with helping one another as well as the folks who came to our little church. I could hear her listenin' to me, but she didn't answer or say anything.

Things went fine for the rest of the day and she sang and played and all until time came to divvy up our earnings and quit for the night. She said she was sorry. It broke my heart 'cause she sounded just like a little girl that'd been chastened and I didn't mean to do that 'cause we've been friends for most of our lives and it's not my lot to judge her, but I'd come to be dependent on her singin' and accordion accompanying and her friendship, and I wanted her to let me help her in whatever way she needed.

She didn't cry. I don't think I ever heard Ginger cry about anything. She's a proud woman like me, but I often break down and cry sometimes when I'm bearing more than my share of trouble or when someone I don't know is kind to me.

Ginger promised she'd do better and then I heard her head off towards her subway stop a block down the street. It broke my heart and I thought on Ginger all the way home that night and prayed to the Lord to help her since I knew I couldn't.

A few months later when Ginger disappeared, I wrote to David and told him what had happened. Being David, he came to the city and made all kinds of inquires but he couldn't find out anything at all about her whereabouts. I couldn't even tell him what stop she got off at on the Broadway line. I didn't even know if she had one place or many where she stayed.

David spent three days inquiring but it didn't do no good or bring up any trace of my poor Ginger. I tried for a few days singing by myself, but it wasn't the same and it seemed like falsifyin', sellin' records that wasn't just me singing, though they did keep selling, we sold about four or five records a day when we was together.

Oh, how I prayed for my Ginger. Difficult as she could be, I loved that girl. We had crossed so many rivers together in our travels to New York City and then singin' together for all those years. I just wonder if she wore out like workin' people do. I know she was havin' trouble with her digesting and all 'cause she'd talk about it and how at night she'd get stomach cramps that would make it so she couldn't sleep.

Oh Ginger, Where are you now? I miss you, and our little group of faithfuls in Brooklyn miss your cheery harmony singin' and rumpus piano playin'.

Without Ginger there wasn't much point in me keepin' workin'. I could keep preachin' and all at our little church, but our mission and God's message was in the music more than in my few words of encouragement to the faithful. I always said they came for the music and for the sharin' time. Ginger would always say, "I think they come for the doughnuts and the coffee!" That was Ginger!

I had to pray to the Lord to keep me from getting dark and not keepin' to his Word. But I sometimes felt like I couldn't hear his Word and I fell to eating more and spending more time with my dolls. I hardly left my room. On Sundays, half-hearted, I went out to Brooklyn to have our service. I asked the faithful to prayer for Virginia, our Deaconess of Music, 'cause I hadn't heard from her for eight weeks.

I preached a sermon about how, when I was a little girl, my stepmother would say, "I don't want a baby in my home. You're not my baby and I never asked for you. You're not wanted here."

I had tears in these dead eyes as I preached on that memory.

And I continued on, saying, "And when I was six years old, my stepmother'd say, 'I didn't ask for no hulk of a young girl living here. Why do you stay here? You eat my food. You sleep on my couch. You know you're not wanted here. Why do you stay?'"

"'Course she kept me 'cause she wanted the state check ever' month. Maybe she thought I'd leave on my own and she'd keep gettin' the check. I'll never know. But it was hard always bein' told I didn't belong and wasn't wanted 'cause, at six and blind and all, I wouldn't've had nowhere to go."

"So, I had to ask myself as a little girl, 'Who does want you? Who will take care of you?' And the only answer that came up for me then was *me, myself, and I*."

"I'd have to be the person to took after and take care of me 'cause no one else was gonna, and that's how it's been and we're here today together in our little church to take care over ourselves, and God is here with us today to help us do that, to be kind to one another and minister unto one another's trials and tribulations, 'cause God knows we have 'em, don't we."

And my six folks sittin' there in their chairs and rockin' back and forth the way us blind folks do all said "Amen, Sister Baybie, amen."

It was one of my best sermons and we all then enjoyed our sharing time together, and coffee and doughnuts, but we was all sad by Ginger not being there with us and we all missed her something terrible.

Wasn't long after the church was condemned and locked up by the city.... I went out one Sunday for our service, 'course I'd get there early to sweep up and all and warm up the old coffee-maker, but when I got there, there was a new lock on the door and I asked a little Negro boy who lived nearby who'd always ask me questions and ask me if he could work for our church for money... I asked him if he saw anything and he said there was a big sign on the door but he couldn't read the writing.

So I asked him if he could read me the letters on the biggest words on the sign and he knew his letters pretty well and read, "T-h-i-s b-u-i-l-d-i-n-g c-o-n-d-e-m-n-e-d b-y t-h-e- B-o-r-o-u-g-h- o-f B-r-o-o-k-l-y-n. N-o O-c-c-u-p-a-n-c-y P-e-r-m-i-t-t-e-d."

I never felt so defeated. First Ginger gone, then our little church we'd taken so much comfort from one another in, and me a licensed preacher in the State of New York and all and no church anymore.

It felt like everything ended at once and for the first time in a long time, I felt like the Lord had abandoned me like my stepmother wanted to do. I retreated into my room, my big chair, my food, and my dolls.

'Course David couldn't leave his work so he'd had to go back to Vermont after he couldn't find Ginger, but he promised to come back in a few weeks. I had a little bit of money saved up 'cause we'd made a lot of money selling records. That usually doubled what we earned in a day singin'. It was like manna from heaven as the Bible says.

That record also opened street folks up sometimes. Usually a person would come by and just drop a coin or sometimes a bill into my cup and back away and leave. I'd thank them with a nod and beam 'em a smile and sometimes a "May the Lord bless ya," 'cause I was always singin'.

If they saw our record leanin' in my lap and wanted to buy one, they'd wait 'til Ginger and me finished our song. Then they'd ask on how much the record cost and I'd tell them and they'd sometimes asked how we'd come to make a record and all and Ginger and I would explain about David and his record company likin' our songs.

The record brought people to us in a way we'd never known before 'cause folks just don't talk to buskers, especially blind ones if my Ginger was right about the sex diseases and all she said about that.

It was a nice change in our work sometimes talking with the people who gave us money and tellin' on how we came to make the record, and 'course when they got to talkin' like that, you could hear 'em begin to fish around in their wallet or their purse for the seven dollars.

It was a welcome change from all those years just feeling different from the people giving us money to talking with them about this and that. The record opened a door for us, as good things in life so often do.

But, oh, how I miss my Ginger today and worry on what became of her. I sometimes like to imagine that some rich person took her into their home and gave her her own room with a private bath, a big piano, and a big tub like they had at the studio, and all the good food she could eat, and there was someone like Sara and Dr. John and his friend Priscilla to care for her like they did and to let her know she was loved and safe. We all want that don't we? That girl deserved more happiness in her life than the Lord ever gave her. I can hear her sweet harmonies today in my mind like she was standin' right next to me.

After I told Eddy what had happened, he brought me an old Victrola his daughter had that played the new album records. He carried it up to my apartment for me and plugged it in and showed me how to use it with the record so I could listen again to Virginia and me singing.

Fuuny how a person's small kindness just always seems to overwhelm me and I cry and cry. That night I stayed up and just listened again and again to Ginger and me singing together and thought the well of tears in me would just dry up, but it didn't.

The two most important women in my life live inside me today, but how I've missed them in my life. I never felt so alone, like the Lord'd abandoned me. But there I go feelin' sorry for myself and not thinkin' on all those who have troubles much worse than my own to bear.

Well, New York didn't leave much for me anymore and I felt like I'd lived out my time there and should maybe go back home, but 'course I didn't know what or where home was. Kansas and Missouri's the only other places I ever lived, but I had no idea how to reach the members of my half-this, step-that family and whether any of 'em was even still on this earth. Almost 25 years had passed since I left.

I worried that I didn't have it in me to move back there and start a new home and all, but I knew I couldn't end my life in this small room surrounded by old men who couldn't even pee straight. I thought maybe if I went back, I could join a small church and solo sometimes with the choir and that I would have a fellowship again and make new friends.

But then I'd get to thinkin' about packin up my stuff and findin' someone to help me figure out the bus schedule and all, and makin' the trip by myself and findin' a new home and it'd just make me feel alone and old.

When Ginger and me was young, we had the spunk and no experience, so we'd just set out and face whatever came, but I'd lived long enough now to imagine on what it would take to start over back in Missouri once I got there.

After a few more weeks alone in my room, I packed up what I could fit in my old suitcase, got a small refund on my weekly rent, 'cause I always had to pay a week ahead, even though I'd been there for so many years, and took a bus home to Kansas City.

Baybie lives in a trailer behind the dump in Licking, Missouri, out on State Highway C. Her neighbor Floyd lives in a nearby trailer and works at South Central Correctional facililty. Floyd's trailer is perpendicular to hers so he can't look in her windows. At least that's what Baybie says. Baybie moved back to Missouri several months after Virginia disappeared. Floyd sees to her needs when he's sober enough.

Baybie's sightless imagination still limns an image of her daughter that stays with her every day and grows, as the years pass, into the image of a lovely young woman. The woman she imagines comes from her days at the School for the Blind, where tactile classroom exercises designed to impart dimension and character to facial features helped students imagine one another's appearance. She has pieced together this image of her daughter also from the many after-lights-out nights in the School for the Blind where she and Anna would continue to explore one another's faces and bodies in an effort to weave an image from curious fingers.

Like many of the girls, Baybie was given a ragdoll to hold until the postpartum yearning subsided, but it never did for Baybie and she was allowed to take the doll with her when she left the home. Baybie still keeps the small ragdoll and the thirty-four other dolls she has collected over the years. The tattered doll was with her when she moved into a trailer provided by Missouri Welfare in 1982. Floyd, also had a welfare trailer, and had been hired to clean and repair Baybie's as best he could with the modest resources supplied by Jim Willis, the case-worker. He replaced the burst pipes that had frozen, leaving them empty until Baybie moved in. He primed the water pump and got the water running again when she moved in, and painted the inside of the trailer with some leftover paint, knowing full well that Baybie couldn't see his work but that Jim would.

Baybie is 72 now and still lives alone in her trailer. The east end of the trailer has settled into the sandy loam and is no longer level. She has learned not to set eggs or round things on her kitchen counter or dining room table.

As in her brief time in Vermont, it was difficult at first for Baybie to get used to the silence. The "firmament sound" is now augmented by the occasional gurgling sounds inside her as she struggles to digest the food that comes her way. Sounds that in the city were buried in the perpetual din of cars and people moving about sometimes jolt Baybie now, like the sound of Floyd slamming the door to his trailer, or the cracking sound of branches in a high wind, and the scurrying sound of mice, chipmunks, and squirrels foraging in the insulated walls of her trailer. Baybie doesn't like the idea that she is sharing her new home with rodents and hopes they are trapped in the walls and cannot get inside.

Floyd sometimes rescues discarded dolls from the nearby dump and Baybie restores them as best she can and cares for them as she remembers being cared for first by her grandmother, and later at the St. Louis and Kansas Schools for the Blind and finally, by Aldo, Lewis, Eddy, and David in New York. She thinks often of her Ginger and wonders if she is still alive too. She still has the Victrola and a stash of records, but the needle is worn away and no longer reaches deep enough into the tiny vinyl grooves to bring Virginia back.

She tries not to think about her time with the Desmets and the awful things that happened in that Godforsaken farmhouse in the middle of nowhere and how Mrs. Desmets then blamed it all on her, as if she had brought it all down on herself. She has almost forgotten the smells and tastes that still make her bilious. She erases the awful taste and smell with a jelly doughnut from her cupboard and a cup of hot cocoa.

The image of her daughter is always with her, especially when she caresses a doll from her collection in her expanding lap. She sees in her mind's eye the beautiful daughter the nurse described to her with her dark brown hair.

It's harder now for Baybie to walk. Like most blind people, she has keen proprioception. She can still sense where her aching limbs are relative to the familiar objects in her trailer. She can walk securely into the kitchen, open a cupboard and reach for a cookie and return to her lounger, avoiding the familiar objects along the way. Lanny and Floyd have learned never to move objects inside Baybie's trailer when they drop by for coffee. Before they knew this, they would be surprised when Baybie asked, "Please put that back where it was when you're done."

Baybie is ponderous now and sways from side to side as she moves about in her trailer. She rarely goes out except when Floyd takes her to see a doctor for an infrequent complaint.

Some nights Lanny stops by when he is done washing dishes at Gert's diner. Lanny met Baybie in church when she first moved back to Missouri and attended the River of Life Full Gospel Church. He plays an old Fender guitar with a tube amp and a plywood speaker box he made from two 10-inch speakers he salvaged from discarded wood console radios. Lanny would accompany Baybie in church on the few occasions when she was invited to sing for the faithful.

Now, she has no ride to church since Floyd no longer does his trading in town at Casey's General Store on Sunday. His truck uses more gas than his old VW that recently "screwed the pooch," as he's fond of saying when any of his meager possessions fail.

Lanny comes by on Monday nights with his Fender and together they have a hymn sing. Lanny's in his early thirties and has worked at Gert's since he was sixteen.

He loves his work. Gert, the owner and cook, lets him take as much leftover food as he wants for himself and for his friend Baybie, so he usually shows up with an old plastic refrigerator drawer covered with wax paper and full of mashed potatoes with gravy, meatloaf, uneaten bread and partial butter pats, drying up custards and sometimes Jell-o squares. Some nights he doesn't come if it's raining. His "beater," as he calls it, can't manage the slurry of muddy gravel road leading up to Baybie and Floyd's trailers. Lanny is large like Baybie and doesn't like to walk, and he doesn't want to get his tube amp wet.

Baybie's other source of food is the Licking Bakery Thrift Store where day-old baked goods are sold for less than a third of their fresh price. Baybie likes the sweet, gooey buns, doughnuts, and melt-in-your-mouth table rolls that Floyd drops off even though the delights they bring her punish her later with a "sour stomach." She learned from Jim that a glass of warm water with a tablespoon of baking soda and some sugar reduces the sharp pain in her stomach after eating her baked goods. She jokes with Lanny and Floyd about the "burp of relief," a phrase she once heard in an antacid ad on her Zenith.

Sometimes when she is savoring a pastry she imagines she's feeding her daughter and the sweet taste in her mouth is an anodyne for the bitter memories and tastes of her own childhood.

Baybie knows that the food she eats is making her ever larger and sicker, but she has given up trying to resist the warmed-over sweet rolls and gravy-covered meatloaf and potatoes that comprise most of her meals alone or with Lanny.

Occasionally, she has what she calls a "food memory" of the oranges the girls were given on the weekends as they whiled away the time waiting for their babies to come full-term. She learned to peel the fruit and to anticipate and savor the tangy sweet flavor of the orange segments.

She remembers once being given a slice of fresh pineapple and chewing the pulp until the last bit of delicious flavor was gone. The nurse had told the girls that fresh fruit was important for the development of their babies. She asked the nurse where the fruit came from and the nurse described an island surrounded by blue sea and sand, which Baybie tried to imagine, but couldn't.

When she was in Kansas City School for the Blind, a teacher had used what she called "synesthesia" to try to evoke a sense of color in the blind girl's imaginations. She would play instruments of the orchestra on a 78 record and relate their sound to various colors. Brown was a bassoon or cello, blue was a trumpet, purple was a French horn, green was a cello. The exercise had fascinated Baybie, but left her with little sense of color other than black and white, the meaning of which she had largely gleaned from her Braille Bible. The timbre of the instruments evoked emotion, but did little to help her form a sense of unique colors.

She likes the wooden crate of Mac apples Floyd brings her in the fall. The tangy juice of the crisp apples causes a sharp pain in her jaw as she lets the juice drip down her throat. She also likes the apples because they don't bring on her sour stomach. In fact, for the month they are in season, she often uses them instead of the baking soda for relief. When they begin to get mushy she no longer eats them though, and Floyd leaves them outside to attract the deer he shoots from his front stoop.

Baybie daydreams a lot and often wonders what kind of family got her Anna. Her experience at the Desmets' had emboldened her to ask someone at the Brill how they chose parents for the babies born there. She was told not to worry about that, but she often does.

She remembers the flavor of vegetables as well, but not with as much pleasure as she remembers the fruit. Sometimes Lanny brings by leftover vegetables, but they are few and far between and often have the acrid taste of the tins in which they are stored.

Baybie's favorite visitor is Ruth Farr, who occasionally drops by with what she called her "fer-laters," leftovers also, but usually full of flavors that Baybie does not recognize, but savors. She will ask Ruth about the spices she uses and the foods that go into her exotic lasagna and lamb stews both of which are marked by the unfamiliar flavor of cloves and nutmeg. Spices other than salt and pepper are alien to Baybie, so Ruth's efforts to make a guessing game of what has gone into them usually stumps her friend.

Baybie and Ruth also met singing in church where they both were drawn to one another's voices and found common cause in their favorite hymns. Unlike Virginia, Ruth, too, is a soprano and they spend many nights trying out different harmonies together, with Lanny playing chords on his Fender. On nights when Floyd is conscious, he can hear the music coming from Baybie's trailer.

Ruth has taught Baybie many traditional hymns from the Baptist tradition and they always open their hymn-sings with her favorite, the "Eternal Rest Hymn:"

Time's clock is striking the hour, Jesus will soon descend,
Clothed in the garments of power, the reign of sin to end.
Then will this anthem be ringing like to a mighty flood,
Then 'round the throne we'll be singing, glory and praise to God.

Chorus

Glory, glory to God! Thus will the ransomed sing;
Glory, glory to God, The everlasting King!
Praise Him, alleluia! To that eternal sphere
We are waiting for our translating;
The time is near.

In those bright mansions supernal, death cannot enter there;
Ages on ages eternal his likeness we shall bear.
There will the once brokenhearted rest in the spirit know;
Sorrow forever departed, gladness shall overflow.

Chorus

Sighing forever is ended, foes shall oppress no more;
Voices in worship are blended to Him Whom all adore.
Bathed in the light soft and tender, sealed for eternity,
Praise to the Lamb we will render — worthy of praise is He.

Chorus

Beautiful, wonderful story! Jesus Himself the Light;
There in the kingdom of glory never shall fall the night.
Now I am singing of heaven, while here I wage the strife;
Then will the victors be given crowns of eternal life.

Chorus

Baybie's musical gift to Ruth was an old favorite she and Virginia often sang together that has now become one of Ruth's favorites:

I was a seeker for light in a dark world,
I looked for truth but settled for lies.
I had been blinded, I couldn't see
Till the Star in Bethlehem's sky opened my eyes.

I have seen the Light shining in the darkness,
Bursting through the shadows, delivering the dawn.
I have seen the Light whose holy name is Jesus,
His kingdom is forever; He reigns on Heaven's throne!

There in a manger, an innocent baby;
Who could believe He was the One;
I can believe it, I know it's true;

He changed my life; He is the light; He is God's Son!
I have seen the Light shining in the darkness,
Bursting through the shadows, delivering the dawn.
I have seen the Light whose holy name is Jesus,
His kingdom is forever; He reigns on Heaven's throne!
We must tell the world what we`ve seen today in Bethlehem!
He`s the promised King; we bow down and worship Him!
Worship Christ The King!

I have seen the Light shining in the darkness,
Bursting through the shadows, delivering the dawn.
I have seen the Light whose holy name is Jesus,
His kingdom is forever; He reigns on Heaven's throne!

Ruth has come to understand that, for Baybie, the frequent allusions to light in the hymns they sing together evoke a day when she will see again, as she did for a few minutes after her difficult birth. Baybie talks to Ruth about these things in a way that she and Virginia never had, as their lives and conversations were usually consumed with the practical aspects of their street work and their music.

Increasingly, Baybie has to get up in the middle of the night and make her way into the trailer's tiny bathroom to pee. It seems recently that her nights are an endless series of trundles back and forth to the cold bathroom. She has also noticed that during the day she has to refill her Mason jar of water next to her recliner more and more often from the kitchen tap. Sometimes her thirst seems unquenchable. The scrapes that she often gets on her shins from inadvertently banging into a chair or counter edge heal more slowly now. She observes this as she often leans forward painfully to rub her shins and thighs to alleviate the dull pain in her legs. She feels the little scrapes and notices that they take much longer to scab over and heal. The sweets that Lanny brings now make her feel drowsy, and she often falls into a troubled slumber until she has to rise again to go to the bathroom or to make her "baking soda cocktail."

She also has been waking up with terrible headaches, a dull pain at the base of her skull. They are making sleep increasingly difficult, and Baybie wakes up in the morning still tired from the night before, since the headaches begin shortly after she dozes off. Ruth asks her if her bed is tilted and Baybie remembers that her whole trailer is slightly tilted. Ruth helps her remake her bed the other way so her head is slightly elevated, and the headaches go away.

Hygiene, too, is more difficult. The pendulous apron of yellow fat over her thighs makes toilet hygiene impossible now. Without saying why, she asked Lanny to bring her one of his soft-bristle bottle brushes from his dishwashing station at Gert's with which she tries to keep clean, but it is increasingly hard as her joints become stiffer and her range of motion decreases.

The vent in her bathroom is rusted shut so the plentiful heat from her kerosene stove does not reach in there. In the winter it is often too cold for her to shower. Besides, the shower stall is not made for a large woman and she finds it difficult to move at all once she's in it. She remembers with a smile the large old porcelain tubs at the School for the Blind and the ten minutes each girl was allowed each week to luxuriate in the warm soapy water that smelled of lye and exotic perfume. There is no bathtub in her trailer and Baybie knows she could no longer get in or, more important, out of a tub.

In late March, a home health nurse comes by. Baybie hears the knock on the aluminum clad trailer door and trills, "Come in, Floyd," though the knock is not like Floyd's brazen hammering. She can usually tell by the time of the visit who is at the door, and besides there is only Floyd, Lanny, and Ruth who visit her. The door opens uncharacteristically slowly. She can hear by the slower squeaks of the three rusty hinges. A new voice introduces itself. "Hi, my name's Jeannie and I'm the new home health nurse. I came to check on you and to see how you're faring. It's been a long winter."

Baybie's response is a mixture of relief and anxiety. The nurses she remembers for the most part were kindly and benevolent and she relishes the idea of being cared for again in some way, especially as it's now harder for her to care for herself. The introduction of a possible new friend is likewise heartening, but will the nurse bring her bad news?

The nurse is shy and asks Baybie questions no one has ever asked her before. She looks at the scars on her legs, asks about the leg pain and how often she urinates. She asks Baybie how often she bathes. Baybie can hear her writing on a pad and asks, "You're not gonna make me move are ya?" The young nurse assures her that she is only checking on her health in an effort to see how she might help Baybie.

Jeannie's hand touches her wrist gently, probes her wrist for a pulse and Baybie feels herself relax. She relishes the gentleness of Jeannie's fingers probing her wrist for an artery and imagines herself touching her baby's tiny wrist.

The questions Jeannie asks are embarrassing, though they are not meant to humiliate Baybie. But she is not proud and knows that her health is declining as more weight accumulates on her aging frame. Her blindness has honed her ability to sense kindness, aggression, disdain, or hostility in the tone of the voices she hears. The tone of Jeannie's questions conveys to Baybie a sense of her innate kindness. But Baybie is still not used to being asked about herself, other than the obligatory "How ya doin?" she hears from Floyd and Lanny, to which she knows they want only one answer, or none.

Jeannie leaves with a promise to return the following week unless a predicted late-March storm hits. She leaves with a vial of Baybie's sugar-rich urine, a blood sample, and a mental note to bring Baybie some fruit.

Baybie is sad to hear her new friend go. She rarely cries, but the experience of being touched and talked to with such tenderness again overwhelms her. She knows this is how she would have been with her daughter. With her sightless eyes overflowing with tears, she abandons herself to the sobs that heave up from deep inside her. She rises painfully and retrieves one of her favorite dolls from the bookshelf.

Neither Baybie nor Floyd have phones, so anyone wishing to talk with Baybie must make the drive up the washed-out gravel drive lined with gray birch trees and knock on the door of her slanting trailer. Nor does Baybie have a mailbox. If Baybie gets any mail other than that addressed to "occupant," Bea, the postmistress, delivers it to Floyd. She doesn't receive any mail though.

Baybie doesn't like the radio preacher. She tells Ruth that he has a "know-it-all voice" and "can't sing to save his soul." She listens just for the familiar hymns his choir sings, though less and less often.

The old hymns of her youth with their emotive metaphors are disappearing from the program's repertoire, replaced by "wishy-washy nonsense like you'd hear coming from behind the curtains in a funeral home," declares Ruth, who sometimes listens with Baybie in the evening when they are finished singing together.

Baybie has not seen Jim Willis since she first moved to Licking four years ago but remembers his many kindnesses and his craggy face, as he had been comfortable letting Baybie touch his features when they first met. His office has since been replaced by a statewide system of social welfare. Gone are the poor farms and overseers who saw to those in need when Baybie was a young woman. Gone too, supposedly, is the stigma of being under their care, but the blight of poverty has by no means been eliminated in the rural countryside.

Baybie's pleasure at Jeannie's visits is increasingly diminished by the continuum of bad news the nurse brings her about her health. She has "the sugar" and will have to have daily shots. She'll have to lose weight and give up the diet of day-old, comfort-pastries that nourish her soul if not her body. Jeannie brings her some lotions for the sores on her legs and a special appliance to better manage her personal hygiene. She's often troubled by the smell of her own body, which she masks with sprinkles from a perfume Ruth brought her. She's given up on the shower, but washes herself as best she can by the kitchen sink when she's alone. She worries that Floyd's watching her the way her Mr. Desmets used to. Floyd, however, can no longer see well enough to shoot the deer in his front yard.

On Jeannie's next visit, she brings a doctor from town who works for the health service. Baybie is surprised when Doctor Menard, greets her in the deep alto voice of a middle-aged woman. She didn't know that women could be doctors and says so with a smile. Dr. Menard is gracious and says with evident pleasure that nowadays some nurses are men. The smile on Baybie's face subsides. She likes Jeannie and doesn't want her replaced by a man.

Jeannie takes Baybie's blood pressure and listens to her heart while Doctor Menard explains to Baybie that she is sick and needs hospital care. Her diabetes is far advanced and her blood sugar, blood pressure, and cholesterol are all too high. Her gums are badly deteriorated and the infection is causing heart problems.

Baybie does not understand any of this and listens fearfully while her hands gather wool quietly below her breasts. She is manipulating something in her imagination. She is with her infant daughter now and wonders, "What will happen to her if I die? Will my daughter have to go to a foster home, as I had to?"

The gentle continuo of Dr. Menard's almost tenor voice recedes in the aural landscape and Baybie imagines herself playing with her daughter by the tiny brook where she and Anna often played as young girls at the St. Louis School for the blind. The sound of the water burbling through the rocks, the smell of the ferns, and the distant lowing of cows overtake the human voices by her side.

The doctor and nurse are gone now and Baybie is alone with her daughter. Baybie explains the sounds and smells to her, though she is not blind. Baybie's fingers comb through her long dark hair. Her soft hands read the high cheekbones and gentle thrust of her daughter's forehead that make for her great beauty. The sounds and smells of this place always summon her daughter to her side until sleep or a knock at the door intervenes.

As the pastoral reverie fades and she remembers the scary words of the doctor, Baybie rises painfully and fetches a break-off from a foil tin of day-old glazed buns drying in her cupboard. Her fingers feather them lightly to make sure no roaches are sharing her snack. Her mouth is dry of late and it is harder to chew the dried-out buns, but she still savors the sweet glaze on the top as the image of her daughter recedes and the crumbs pile up on her breasts.

She remembers Jeannie telling her that they will come for her tomorrow. She remembers Jeannie's promise to stay by her side during the trip to the hospital.

Baybie is apprehensive. Her "sour stomach" returns with a vengeance and she can feel the acid rise in her gorge as she continues to pull off and eat pieces of her pastries. She yearns for the taste of a tart apple or a juicy sweet orange. She misplaced the two pears Jeannie brought her and cannot remember where she left them, though her trailer is redolent with the smell of their ripening.

Her daughter is with her more now in her imagination and she pays less attention to her dolls. The rubbery faces, stiff fabrics, and bristly synthetic hair she palpates and strokes conflict with her image of the many children to whom she has given birth in her imagination. Her children are very much alive, but it is to her eldest daughter she returns most often for solace and understanding. The others are too young and she knows they should not be burdened with her earthly cares. Her oldest daughter understands and is with her.

Jeannie arrives the next day with an orderly and a large wheelchair into which the man helps Baybie. She asks Jeannie to tell the man not to help her, but just to push the chair. She takes the few fearful steps from her lounger to the oversize chair and falls back into it. She hears and smells the orderly's breath as he approaches to fold down the metal platforms for her feet. He must move her legs out of the way to do this, and takes hold of her right leg. She cries out and asks Jeannie not to let him touch her. Jeannie takes over and gently moves Baybie's swollen legs and lowers the footplates. The orderly is strong and guides the chair from behind down the cinderblock stairs Floyd built. The orderly cannot understand her reticence, but has learned his place in the world of the sick and the infirm.

It is many years since Baybie has been in a car. She notes the comfort of the seat, unlike the hard bench seats she remembers. The car is quieter, too. She senses the smaller interior proportions and wonders if cars are smaller now inside or whether she is just larger. She touches the glovebox and dash panel on the passenger side and does not know what she is touching, nor does she ask. She does not want the orderly driving the car to infer a relationship.

Baybie is astounded at her hospital bed. It is unlike the dry foam mattress in which she sleeps at night with its depression in the middle. This bed is firm yet comfortable. The sheets are ironed and crisp and she loves to pull them up over her chin on which she has recently felt a few hairs growing. She can move the backrest and the part under her knees up and down and does so to reduce the dull aches in her lower back and legs. She confides to Jeannie that she does not want to go home again.

Floyd and Lanny come by for a visit, and so does Ruth. When Ruth enters her room, she smells the inviting scent from the basket of fruit she has brought. She is touched that Ruth remembers her fondness for fruit.

"Jeannie told me it was okay to bring you some fruit and that it's good for you, so I brought some." Ruth offers to cut some up and they share a couple of ripe peaches.

Baybie is delighted to hear Ruth's voice and they chatter on about events. Baybie asks Ruth about Floyd, who was caught jacking deer again and has lost his precious hunting license. She had grown used to the sharp reports as Floyd tried in vain to sight in his rifle behind his trailer in the woods. Lanny has started a country rock band and is back on the day shift at Gert's.

Baybie revels in the news of her friends, all the while inhaling the alluring scents of the fruits being pared and sliced. Ruth wraps Baybie's hands around a cool porcelain bowl with a fork in it. Baybie lifts the bowl to her nose and inhales deeply, smiling. She tries to envisage the fruits that exhale such beautiful aromas. She forks up slices at random and asks Ruth to tell her what they are as she brings them to her mouth so she can relate the bursts of flavor to the name of the fruit in case she might ever ask for them again.

The exotic flavors bring tears to her eyes. She wishes she had known these flavors earlier. The two she savors most are the ripe peach and cantaloupe. She rolls these around in her mouth and tries to imagine the size and shape of the fruit, where it might have come from. She regrets that she cannot share their flavor and aroma with her daughter.

Baybie finishes the fruit, thanks Ruth and, for old time's sake, she and Ruth sing an old-time favorite called, "Telephone to Jesus".... "Central's never busy, always on the line...."

Unbeknownst to Baybie, faces appear at the door and smile into the private room.

Dr. Menard tells her of the surgery they must perform to save her life and Baybie is consoled by her daughter who has been with her much of the time that she has been alone in the hospital room. She asks her daughter if the loss of her leg will bring an end to the pain it gives her.

Baybie's favorite time is when her daughter gives her a back rub. Baybie lies on her stomach and withdraws the pale pink gown. It is not cold in the hospital room. Baybie can hear Anna rubbing her hands together to warm them up and then hears the splurt of the plastic bottle as it dollops out the warm lotion that prevents more sores from forming. Anna gently warns Baybie that she is about to touch her and Baybie feels the warm lotion slather over her back and the backs of her thighs and the gentle hands of her daughter rubbing the sore flesh. Her anxiety subsides and she basks in the feeling of being touched gently for her own pleasure rather than someone else's.

The day of her surgery, her daughter is again with her. At first when a nurse places the gauze mask over her mouth, she is apprehensive, but Anna assures her that she will stay with her. She follows directions and inhales the air that smells of cleaning fluids.

Anna is holding her hand and talking gently to her the whole time. She leads her mother back to the stream where they have spent so much time together. She can hear the movement of water over rocks in the distance and the sound of cows chewing their cuds. She stops and waits as her daughter picks some blue flowers. She describes their pale blue color and holds them up to her mother's nose. They tickle her nostrils and she can feel their tiny size and smell their faint scent. They settle down on a moss mound near the water's edge. Baybie can again smell the ferns that she has so often rubbed on her cheek to sense their shape, texture, and smell. She lies down and spreads her cotton dress discreetly over her knees even though she knows she is alone with her daughter. It is a matter of habit and she wants to set a good example for her daughter.

After several minutes, her daughter tells her she must go now. Baybie doesn't understand and asks her why she is leaving her alone after all this time together. Her daughter tells her that she loves her, touches her face, and says that she must now go and begin to lead her own life. She tells her mother that she's in a safe place by the water and that no one will ever touch her badly again. Baybie's sightless eyes again fill with tears as she hears her daughter's retreating steps. She wonders if her daughter is looking back at her as she walks away through the rustling ferns.

COLOPHON

Digital printing
by Lightning Source

Typefaces used are Freight
by Joshua Darden/Darden Studio
and BAQ Metal by Thinkdust

Magic Hill Press LLC
144 Magic Hill Road
Hinesburg, VT 05461

www.ingramcontent.com/pod-product-compliance
Lightning Source LLC
Chambersburg PA
CBHW020637250626
47154CB00008B/2720